1

MW01173384

A Historical Novel of Pioneer Life Along the Forks of the Mohican River.

Jason Ireland

Nedjes Books
Mansfield, Ohio

Dedicated to my brother, Nathan Ireland

Acknowledgements

This book, its manuscript written by hand over a decade, would not be possible without the editing and input of my father, David Ireland, whose ability to read my scrawl borders on the supernatural. I would also like to thank my daughters, Morgan and Audrey who spent their earliest years watching their dad pen this work. Most of all I would like to thank my wife, Rose, whose patience and encouragement kept me from shelving this project when the writing was going poorly.

I would like to thank Robert Carter for discussing history with me and giving me the great example of his books.

A special thanks goes to Dan and Janet Rhodebeck for their expertise in editing historical writing. Also Dr. Barbara McGovern, now deceased, for reading and marking my first draft, and for discussing my project with me when I wasn't sure where it was headed, propelling its evolution.

I would like to thank all of the archivists, historians and friends who answered my questions and read drafts of this book. I am so grateful—Jason Ireland

Copyright © 2018 by Jason Ireland
All rights reserved

Contents

Part One

Part Two

Introduction

"Nothing happened here!" So said my high school History teacher when I asked about Richland County's connection to the war of 1812. We had just finished watching a black-and-white film short on Perry's victory near Put-in-Bay, the first time the British navy surrendered a squadron of its ships to a foreign power. It was an American victory, accomplished on an inland lake surrounded by a vast unbroken wilderness, while 50 miles to the south militiamen gathered around a rude blockhouse (one of two that marked the edge of Mansfield commons) where they strained to hear faint echoes of the cannonade.

Today traffic noise alone would prevent hearing cannons on Lake Erie. Not far from the city square stands one surviving blockhouse, relocated for its own safety, rescued from the bustle of urban life. This unique relic is preserved as it should be, though its past is poorly understood by most.

I am amused as I conclude research for this book that my teacher, had he stood on the site of my school in 1812 would have witnessed up-close the sad removal of the Delaware from Greentown, their camp being just over the hill from the parking lot. And, had you stood on the site of Mansfield Senior High (my father's alma mater) during this time you would have heard shots that brought down the Wyandot Toby before he was tomahawked to death in the creek below what is now the bike trail.

For most of us, our local history consists of a jumble of disconnected facts and tales dispersed among Ohio History books and various roadside markers. But through letters, documents and books one can hear a faint whisper of the voices from the wilderness, their stories revived and retold by those who knew and survived them, carefully adjusted for the attitudes of their time.

So it is that this information begs re-examination every century or so. As a student of History I make no attempt to put a modern spin on the past, but to pen unpolished a collection of these tales, free of contemporary morality and politics. Through the vehicle of fiction we become flies on the wall, witnesses to the conversations of the time. It is my hope that in gathering material from diverse sources, I can open a window to the past and engage the curiosity of the student, young or old, who asks "What happened here?" as well as provide a resource for further inquiry and investigation.

Jason Ireland

Prologue

Spring 1808

John Gilkison, Quartermaster and vanguard of George Larwill's surveying party, awoke gasping on the floor of his makeshift home inside the hollow base of an ancient sycamore tree. Thick smoke from a small fire kindled just outside to discourage wolves and ease the chill, swelled his eyelids nearly shut as he began choking on the noxious fumes, which swirled in a downdraft. Outside in the inky blackness of an early morning storm an unknown assailant ransacked the staging point that he and George Coffinberry cleared from the wilderness the night before.

Bears! Bears, common here, were their fiercest during mulberry time when they tutored their unfledged young on the basics of feeding. Forced to ignore this hazard, Gilkison burst through the fire in a dive while at the same time cocking the pistol he had cradled throughout the night. His arm was suddenly grabbed, flipping him on his back then dragging him clear of danger.

It was a rescuer. "John!" shouted a voice through the black smoke. "Dammit John are you alright?" "I never took you for such a fool, John," growled George Coffinberry as he helped the gasping Gilkison to his feet. "And to think I let such a foolish man marry my daughter," he said only half joking. "Sometimes it is best to go without a fire as you well know."

"Anything in the snares?" asked Gilkison eager to change the subject.

"Not one damned thing." spat Coffinberry searching his filthy waistcoat for a plug of tobacco. "Larwill found the hind quarter of a deer carcass not ten rods down that old Indian path." he said pointing into the dissipating rain. "I told him that if we held our noses it could be nourishing but he elected to throw it in the trap—figures the bear might be back for it."

For the last three days and nights neither of them had eaten meat, subsisting instead on berries and crawfish, both preferring hunger to depleting their supply of hard tack in order to guarantee provisions for the stragglers scheduled to rendezvous with them on the broad spring-fed hummock that Larwill dubbed "Mansfield square."

"I sometimes wonder," groused Coffinberry, "if our esteemed Mr. Mansfield even knows of the hellish tangle he lent his name to."

"Bureaucrats," replied Gilkison, "will plant their flag on a dung heap if it suits their purpose." One-by-one the rest of the party wandered into camp looking the worse for wear. Without invitation, they descended upon the last of Gilkison's stores.

"You might as well have feasted last night!" shouted Larwill, kicking over the ration bag, around which a puddle had formed. "It's all turned to paste." The surveyor, now livid, cursed the rain and Gilkison again before ducking into a tarpaulin hastily strung over a fallen tree for his comfort.

"The only ones at camp with full bellies are the ants and beetles." observed Coffinberry who, having suffered through the worst of the War of Seventy-Six, and being the eldest of the party, was the only one seeming to enjoy the whole ordeal. "I believe, Mr. Gilkison, that we have among us the fattest cockroaches in all the land." he added with a smile.

"Don't eat them." mumbled John Chapman who winced as he looked for something solid in the ration bag. Coffinberry prepared to kindle a new fire using coals from the old one inside a stove-in  barrel with stones in the bottom. He propped it at an angle against a log to keep out the incessant drizzle. "Yes, yes this is how we kept warm at Trenton in the Spring of Seventy-Eight—rained for two weeks straight," he expounded to the annoyance of all. The rekindled fire grew, radiating its nurturing warmth, as smoke spiraled upward like a dancer in celebration, accompanied by a chorus of birds and frogs.

"I hope there is something boiling-hot to drink. What say you Mr. Coffinberry?" announced Winn Winship upon his arrival (and in his usual stilted bray). His powdered wig, tucked under his arm, was filled with berries. "I should hope I am not the only one who met with some success." he said, dumping his gleanings on the mottled earth where the party sat. The humor of his wig being filled with fruit where his brains normally reside was not lost on the others, but no one laughed. "Humph." He sighed, stuffing the battered hairpiece, worth half-a-month's wages, into his waistcoat.

"You should return that thing to the wild before its mother comes looking for it." snickered Coffinberry, able to maintain a serious demeanor no longer. Winship, a genteel anomaly in the wilderness broke into a genuine self-deprecating grin and looked around the camp.

"I think I shall erect my cabin here." Winship declared. "It is not as miasmic as the lowlands to be sure."

"You? Build here?" repeated Gilkison with a snort. "I can't imagine such a thing."

"And why not?" interrupted Winship, "After all, I am Postmaster of this place."

"I guess this puts us square in your parlor, Winship." added Larwill, handing him an open bottle of metheglyn. "But is this how you plan to entertain?" Winship took a good swig, gagging on its harsh bite.

"Not at present!" he hacked, stooping awkwardly into the old sycamore. "I think I'll retire to the bed chamber, for when I awaken, I shall expect a city complete with spires and a Main Street."

"Of course, of course." replied Larwill. "We'll start after breakfast."

Brownstown Creek

Michigan Territory

1812

The seam of William McCullough's jacket collar was split open as a tomahawk buried itself in his neck up to the handle, sending him off his mount teeth-first toward the hard–packed trail. Birds and rabbits scurried as a cacophony of war whoops and shrill bone whistles pierced the dense tangle along the path. Suddenly, the tree line erupted with the uneven crackling of musketry and the yells of advancing braves.

"It's a trap" screamed Major Van Horne stepping over the convulsing McCullough and leveling his pistol at the chest of a charging warrior. With a sharp squeeze of the trigger, he dropped his opponent beneath a cloud of smoke. Lead zipped around the soldiers like angry bees, splintering low hanging branches overhead. Militiamen shot wildly, some throwing down their weapons before splashing across the shallow creek.

George McCullough knelt over his brother cupping the shattered skull in both hands. His lips were moving, quivering the way they used to when he was a child being scolded. The flash of renewed volleys soon pulled his attention elsewhere as Van Horne shouted a warning. Before McCullough could get his bearings, the cries surrounding him had changed from those of his comrades to those of Shawnees. He rose and spun around only to catch the blur of a warrior coming at him with club held high. All he could do was deflect the blow, thrusting his rifle high overhead. Seeing his chance, the warrior lunged toward McCullough, bashing his stomach with the end of a mace, doubling him over.

 Two shots in succession, spun the attacker around, spattering McCullough with blood. Samuel Morrison kicked the dying Indian off of the disbelieving McCullough who he helped to his feet. "The Goddam Major took off with most of the men" said Morrison. "We got to flee boy, right now."

Morrison threw down his broken rifle and pulled a loaded pistol from William McCullough's lifeless body. They scrambled across the flood plain, through the brush, over the banks and down into Brownstown Creek, where the freezing water forced them to gasp for breath, as Morrison dragged McCullough across the rushing stream. All fighting had stopped. The Shawnee, ecstatic in their great victory, were dancing among the bodies of their slain and dying enemies.

Suddenly, a pair of mounted warriors sprang from the commotion like crazed wolves stalking the struggling soldiers. Exhausted, McCullough stumbled behind the trunk of a great oak, pulling

Morrison down with him. "Stay still; we have no chance in the open," whispered McCullough, unsheathing his knife. Morrison looked down at the pistol shaking in his hands. "My God, we have only one shot between us."

The Shawnees dismounted, drawing their tomahawks before vaulting over the moss-covered tree trunk. Morrison sprang to his feet, aiming his pistol at the young warrior's torso, then pulling the trigger. With a snap, the hammer struck the frizzen, failing to create a spark. The charging brave swung his tomahawk, chopping into Morrison's left shoulder as blood gushed from the wound. Morrison tackled his assailant, slamming him into the tree trunk, then beating him unconscious with the brass pommel of the gun butt. Clutching his wound, he staggered forward and collapsed in a heap before the other two struggling men. The older warrior's foot slipped in the mud as a desperate McCullough lunged, driving his knife to the bone in his attacker's thigh. With a howl, the injured fighter pulled the blade out and stumbled over Morrison, disappearing into the underbrush.

Then there was quiet—only the sounds of running water and swaying branches overhead. McCullough peered over the tree trunk, scanning the far bank for more attackers. The war party had disappeared leaving behind a tangle of naked dead. "William's one of them," he thought turning away from his perch.

A spotted pony somehow remained, its reins thrown over a hickory sapling. He pulled a sugar loaf from his pack and slowly approached the Shawnee mount, locking eyes with it. The pony remained calm and quickly accepted the treat, allowing McCullough to lead it back to the clearing. Morrison opened his eyes, much weakened by the blood loss. He tried to stand, shifting his weight from the left shoulder to his elbow then onto both hands. The young brave was gone leaving behind a dark patch of blood.

"We best leave, Samuel," hissed a voice from behind. Morrison turned around to find McCullough with the restless pony. McCullough tore off the bottom of his undershirt and used it as packing for Morrison's shoulder. "Nearest blockhouse is miles from here. I hope you can make it," said McCullough grimly as he assisted Morrison to his feet. "Give me that pony and I'll make it just fine," replied Morrison.

Whatever warmth mid-day had provided vanished with the setting sun, as a profound chill set in. McCullough took a kerchief from his pack and tied it snugly over his sunburned face. The pony seemed to guide itself through the wooded expanse toward a chimney of smoke rising from the Garrison stockade. When they finally arrived at the stockade gate, Morrison slumped precariously over his mount, oblivious to the sentry's hail, as McCullough stumbled alongside, burning with fever as troops rushed out to assist the failing men.

Once inside, McCullough was eased onto the floor beside a blazing fire, where he drifted in and out of consciousness. Morrison was placed on a bench and prepared for medical treatment of his shoulder. A surgeon nudged McCullough a bit in order to retrieve instruments from a boiling kettle. Another nudge, followed by a familiar voice in his ear brought McCullough to a confused state. He rubbed his eyes, trying to focus them on the figure looking down at him. "Brother...?" William extended his hands, dropping a gory tomahawk onto McCullough's blanket. The apparition's mouth opened in a ghastly grin revealing a hideous tangle of broken teeth. McCullough shrieked, recoiling from the fading specter. As his eyes began to focus, only the surgeon remained, standing in place of his brother. McCullough looked down at his lap, fumbling through the blanket for the grizzly weapon, finding only a tourniquet clamp. "Sorry I dropped my vice on you," croaked the sawbones. "I am clumsy with drink. This is the damnest year is it not? Frost in June—this cold! Take a dram and get yourselves some rest." McCullough declined the jug, instead propping himself against the warm hearth step. Across the room Samuel Morrison lay sprawled on a log bench, moaning in a fitful sleep. Long matted hair covered his face exposing what was left of a rough-cropped ear. This mark of a thief, ordinarily well hidden beneath his coal black mane, was now uncovered for all to see—and judge.

"Will he live?" asked McCullough.

"Oh, I think," muttered the pock-marked surgeon, who turned his attention back to the jug of brandy. "I looked him up and down after I sewed him back together. He's weathered ugly wounds before—you can see the scars—but only time can tell for sure. Your fever is a different matter; you must look after yourself. I've seen it fell stronger men than you. Ponder that and pray. I'm gonna find my cot and keep warm, lad. You should do the same."

McCullough shifted restlessly on the puncheon floor, his ears trained on each gust that whipped around the rampart walls. In his delirium, he could make out voices in the whistling wind. Mother, sometimes God Himself spoke, their guidance all but lost under the groans of his wounded companion. He closed his eyes and pulled the linsey-woolsy blanket tight around his aching head, silencing the phantoms.

Soldiers gathered near the door, wary of their new messmates' sounds and smells. "These two should be horse whipped—damned cowards," came a voice from the crowd, who entered the room and examined the new arrivals. A young pimple-faced recruit stepped away from the circle of men and lifted the compress on Morrison's shoulder. "Sweet Lord! What the hell happened to him?" The surgeon shifted uncomfortably in his cot, posting himself up on his elbows. "Those two came from Van Horne's command; got cut up near Brownstown, the last to wander in."

The boy moved from Morrison's bench to the tarpaulin knapsack wadded beneath McCullough's head. He smirked, then pulled out an ivory lice comb, licked its fine teeth and ran it through his oily hair. Emboldened he asked, "Where are their muskets?" His smile broadened. "You mean to say Doc, that this trash fought off ole Tecumseh with this here comb?" The others laughed as he held the comb the close to the hearth, frying the lice off its tines then ran it through his hair a second time.

Since hundreds of Van Horne's unit had run or retreated at Brownstown, McCullough and Morrison were suspected of cowardice the day before, by those who were not present at the battle. But the suspicion stopped just short of accusation and the two, though subjected to rudeness, were not arrested, and rejoined their units when their health improved.

An inquiry was held at Fort Detroit, and Morrison and McCullough were summoned. Formal proceedings were rare, intimidating and final. Morrison wrung his hands nervously as he waited to testify. He tried not to dwell on the many punishments reserved for cowards—branding, gibbeting, and, of course, the noose. Never had he been as fearful of the Indians as he was of the officers seated before him. They had assembled that morning at this frontier outpost and were all business. Quietly they conferred, illuminated by open rows of gun ports which cast an eerie glow above their heads. Major Van Horne sat motionless and sullen, partly obscured by smoke from burning pipes and flickering candles. General Hull closed his watch and glanced at the stack of papers before him. His eyes darted quickly from an empty dram glass to McCullough and then to Van Horne. Lastly, he surveyed the crowd in attendance. Major Stevens rose and began the questioning.

"Private Samuel Morrison, it has been stated that Private McCullough and yourself were amongst the last to vacate the skirmish line at Brownstown; am I correct?" Morrison paused before answering in the affirmative. Hull edged his spectacles to the tip of his nose, examining the top paper a second time. "George McCullough, you may step forward," he ordered. "Major Van Horne states that at said engagement his command met with a Native war party three hundred strong outside of Brownstown, where his force was overwhelmed, and ultimately defeated. How many Indians did you witness, roughly?" McCullough approached the bench giving his answer to the General in a hushed tone as if to conceal it from his commanding officer, Van Horne. This angered Major Stevens who stood up pointing the stem of his pipe at McCullough.

"By God you will answer the question in a clear, concise manner for all to hear! Now please proceed."

"We were in the bitter thick of it," replied McCullough uncomfortably, "Morrison, my brother William, and myself. I reckoned there to be twenty, maybe thirty savages at most." The blockhouse erupted with outraged shouting and calls of order as General Hull pulled a polished river stone from his pocket and rapped it loudly on the thick oak table restoring silence to the room.

"Private Morrison, I ask you, what was the enemy's strength, in your best reckoning, when Major Van Horne sounded retreat?"

Morrison searched his memory. "Well, sir, there weren't as many savages as there are men in this room." Morrison fidgeted uneasily. "I cannot speak for the Major, or what he witnessed that day."

Major Stevens interrupted. "We found eighteen dead, from your unit, Mr. McCullough's brother being amongst them. God knows what happened to the seventy others that are missing out of a force two hundred strong. I shall know from Major Van Horne, how this can be!"

General Hull turned flush with anger rapping the gavel stone until his fingers hurt, his shrill voice cutting through the disorder. "Mr. Morrison, Mr. McCullough, you will report to Sergeant Gilkison who will escort you back into Ohio and find a place for you both in Captain Johnston's rifle company. Now get out of my sight before there is protest." Major Stevens grunted his agreement, waving Morrison and McCullough away from the bench. Suddenly, it was over.

John Gilkison sat outside the Blockhouse door, deftly crushing fleas with the heel of his boot. The Sergeant cared little for commissioned officers and their formalities, much less the thought of escorting rabble through the fetid swamps of central Ohio. Two jolts and the door wrenched open expelling McCullough and Morrison into the sunlight.

"They must be saving all the rope for Van Horne," said Gilkison out loud, leafing through his warrants one last time.

Morrison hesitated, stepping away from the brooding Sergeant, then said, "I reckon you're the justice come to take us back to Coshocton—God I hope not in chains."

Gilkison chuckled. "Chains? I'm afraid not. There will be no need for chains in Johnston's command. We are bound for the forks of the Mohican—a sweet haven for idle soldiers and border roughs. There we will put up blockhouses and, God willing, keep the peace for Colonel Kratzer. Should you think of deserting remember the rifle at your back. Keep that in mind and there will be no need for Mr. McCullough here to dig you a grave. Do we have an understanding?"

"There will be no trouble on our parts." replied McCullough unhappily. "It's damn unjust."

"I don't care," interrupted Gilkison testily, "Go tell it to your horse."

Greentown

James Copus watered his horse in a bubbling spring as an advance party of militia marched past him, breaking out of the wilderness. Standing on dry ground was a small comfort thought Copus, having spent the better part of the morning slogging through sludge and water at the swamp's edge. Then, reflecting on the arrival of

 militia in this remote meeting place, he surmised that today's business could not end well. Captain Douglass of the Ohio Militia rode up to the spring, nudging Copus's mount out of the way.

The Captain noticed a look of concern on Copus's face, but dismissed it saying, "Don't worry Reverend; good shall come of this one way or the other." The wily Captain drew his pistol and checked the pan before stuffing it back into his sash. "I suggest you say a prayer that all may go as I have planned. Some of the men are itching for a fight; it's in their stink. No doubt your local boys will behave like Christian saints, but as for the Kentuckians, that's another matter." Without further comment, the Captain galloped off leaving the Reverend Copus trailing behind.

John Gilkison cursed as he shoved undisciplined men back into formation along the main column marching to within sight of the village. Captain Cunningham of Mansfield Settlement issued orders to a red-faced officer, passing him a field glass that seldom left his hand. Native farmers scattered before the militiamen sparking hoots of laughter and cat-calls in the first few ranks. Cunningham rode beside Copus, handing him a bottle of metheglyn that had been circulating among the officers. Copus declined the drink and passed the bottle back.

"Well Reverend, you best have a good nip and catch up with Captain Douglass before he rides into town alone. I do not envy you your task, Reverend. You must try to negotiate for the Governor and your friend, old Chief Armstrong, as well. With Douglass's finger on the trigger; oh I do not envy you, no Sir! You can't serve two masters, they say, at least not these two."

Wisps of smoke rose from fire pits and vanished into the morning fog, as cicadas rasped their calls from treetops on a nearby hill. So blanketed, the Indian village of Greentown was springing to life. A scattering of Delaware women, accompanied by the antiphonal calling of crickets, could be seen rekindling cook fires outside wigwams and log huts that dotted the plateau.

In the great council house, Captain Douglass twisted restlessly in his chair, daubing sweat off his forehead with a handkerchief. Thomas Armstrong, the village leader threw another log on the fire making the room unbearable for Douglass and his delegation. Armstrong paused for a moment looking into the sweating faces around the room. He turned and spoke. "We are peaceful hunters and farmers, nothing more. Let us not quarrel over the British. The harvest is drawing near and without our crops we will not survive the winter." Douglass loosened his collar and took off his uniform coat, then spoke. "Word has it that you and your people are listening to Tecumseh's treachery. I can no longer ignore such accusations. Your neighbors are understandably jittery and a bit trigger-happy as war approaches. You and your people will be removed for the safety of all."

A reluctant mediator, the Reverend Copus swallowed a cup of water before addressing the Delaware Council. "What we desire, by the grace of God, is to live together in peace and unity. This is, after all, a temporary removal for your safety as well as our own." Douglass quietly studied the expressions of the men in the lodge while Armstrong pondered the meaning of the Reverend's words. Kanotchy, one of the council, revealed nothing as he drew smoke from the long stem of an ornate ceremonial pipe, then passed it in turn across the table to the Captain. Kanotchy turned to Copus "Tell him, neighbor, that we have made no treaty with the King or his allies. Go home, leave us to our crops."

Douglass shook his head, passing the pipe to Armstrong. "I do not have the time to separate sheep from goats. You will all leave together or suffer the consequences. Rumor has it there are those among you who have fallen-in with Tecumseh and that you are arming yourselves for war. The Governor has ordered you to leave. You will comply with the Governor's orders, or there will be bloodshed—mark my words!" A chill ran down Copus's spine as he struggled with the gravity of relaying Douglass's warning.

"Captain, putting your message as such a threat—it offends—please! Armstrong and his Delaware harm no one. Our children hunt and play together. We break bread together often."

"I don't want your opinion Copus," snapped Douglass, cutting-off the shaken clergyman abruptly. "One more attempt at obstruction and I will have you arrested." Douglass stood up pointing a finger at the bearskin flap that hung across the threshold. "Outside this doorway there are two companies of militia, taking soup with your wives. Some of the volunteers are little more than savages and will gladly trade a woman's hospitality for scalps and plunder. If the Delaware evacuate peaceably, no harm will come to your kin or their possessions. You have my word as an officer. But, one way or another, you will leave this place today." Douglass produced a piece of paper. "Sign this order and you will be escorted to safety under my protection."

One-by-one, Armstrong and the stony-faced council members made their mark on the document, ignoring any further formalities on the part of Captain Douglass by walking out the door. With a yank, the bearskin door came down and a dozen elderly women entered the lodge, surrounding Douglass and his party, hastily removing every useful item they could carry. Outside the council house Gilkison somberly directed his men as they separated the Delaware into two groups, by gender. They formed a long line, two abreast, while Copus and another soldier persuaded the young braves to put down their brush hooks and pitchforks before the Kentuckians reacted violently. Copus approached young Silas Armstrong, pulling the knife from his hand, replacing it with a full canteen. "Silas, your father needs you now; go with him." The young man returned his gaze with a look of betrayal as a soldier nudged him to the line.

Under a tree, Copus rubbed his eyelids, made swollen by the many extinguishing fires that choked the air with steamy smoke. Next to him James Kinney shut the front piece of his lap desk with a loud bang, distracting Copus' attention from studying the inventory list of household goods left behind, taken at the insistence of the Delaware. Captain Douglass stood nearby, lighting his pipe from the last cook fire. "Reverend, your work here is done. The Greentown Delaware will have ample time to reflect on these consequences along the roads to Piqua." Copus folded the list and handed it to him.

"Captain, the only British contraband reported are a few tin cups, a dozen blankets, and a stew pot." Douglass stepped closer to him and spoke in a low deliberate voice. "Damn it Copus, any British contraband represents an act of war! Do you think the British are just being neighborly? Do you actually believe the Delaware are ignorant of our situation? Reverend, you are dear to the hearts of many in this wilderness. If it were not for your reputation, I would hang you from the whipping post at the Mansfield stockade."

A small boy, straining from the weight of many canteens slung around his neck, cautiously approached Douglass, delivering the Captain's mount. Douglass met his eyes. "You the Sergeant's lad, is it? Straighten up and fill those canteens! When you are finished, put to use that pennywhistle you so often force upon us." Douglass launched himself into the saddle and turned his horse around Copus. "When you have your wits about you, call on me at the at the blockhouse for your compensation." He then doffed his hat, leaving the shaken clergyman under the judging eyes of the captives.

Children milled about in the shadow of the great hill—a giant watching over them since birth. Old men, once venerable warriors, sat atop their ponies, chastising the young for not holding their heads high. From the head of the column Thomas Armstrong's voice could be heard, chanting prayers with the Holy Men as his people left Greentown behind.

The procession began to move, leaving their homes and crops behind, against their will. Two little girls, cousins, tried to keep-up near the rear of the column. Naomi chewed her lower lip, ignoring the pebble grinding at the calloused sole of her foot. She dared not stop or even lose pace with the others, fearing the soldiers bringing up the rear. Lightheaded with hunger, her cousin, Olena, searched her tunic pockets, for what little food she had managed to hide from her captors—three carrot roots and a green potato—just enough she thought for soup should they make camp. Swept up in this exodus, she was only visiting Greentown from her home in Upper Sandusky, where she lived with her father, Toby. Naomi tightened her hold on the buckskin fringe that hung from Olena's frock.

"I do not hear the soldier's feet behind us," gasped Naomi. "Let us sit and remove the pebble." Olena carefully helped her onto a log before easing the moccasin off of her swollen foot. Olena looked over her shoulder, scanning the path, looking all the way to the horizon for militiamen.

Morrison and McCullough had dropped from the rear of the procession as it turned around a hill, and returned to Greentown with several others. "We used to come up this way, through the Blackfork, when I was just a lad with my father," mused Morrison as he swirled his canteen. "In the fall of each year there was a big fur market near the chief's house over yonder. You should have seen it! Squaws would turn out of their lean-tos and decorate the fence posts with woven blankets.

Everything was for sale that week. There was wealth until the trappers and traders left town and moved west. All that was left is this dog patch you see before you."

"I know of a couple of men in Mansfield who will grow fat with wealth after today's events," said McCullough as he peered into a willow coop. Morrison looked irritated and he changed the subject. "If we go missing, no one in that louse town will keep us from the rope." McCullough waved him off stuffing a lifeless hen into his empty mess bag. "We'll catch up Sam, right now hunger motivates me more than the noose. Leave if you like, I am not afraid."

McCullough got a deep satisfaction from setting the first cabin alight. A powerful wind blew the growing inferno from one building to another, and he figured it was a Divine hand bringing justice. He felt like a powerful avenger and was much pleased.

Olena spotted something. Rising ominously from afar she saw thick black smoke. Surprised, she stepped backward nearly knocking Naomi from her perch. "Watch your step, you are bigger than me!" exclaimed Naomi. "What do you see? Are they near?" Olena turned around, stepping over Naomi. "Look! They burned the village. I can see the smoke. We must go quickly and find the others" she said breathlessly. Olena started for the column now long out of sight, sprinting alongside the freshly cut wagon ruts that mired the sunken road. Panting, she paused at the rise of a hill, shaded by a maple tree that soared overhead. In a crevasse between two roots of the tree, water had collected. It was alive with mosquito larvae and small worms. Olena folded a leaf, pushing back the wrigglers, and proceeded to sip water through a hollow reed, then stepped aside while Naomi splashed the remainder on her forehead.

The column remained out of sight. This tree was ideal for climbing and soon provided a high vantage point with a long panoramic view. Six Wyandots came into sight, running in pairs as if in a footrace. From her high perch on a stout limb, Olena watched the unarmed braves approach. She scrambled down to the ground, waving her arms at the party of revenge-seeking braves. Out of breath, Kanotchy slowed his pace allowing the younger men to pass him by. "Toby's daughter; is that you? How many soldiers left for the village?" he asked realizing that soldiers must have split off the line to return to the village and destroy it. Olena pursed her lips and, counting the number on her fingers, said "There were six or eight of them guarding us at the rear of the line. They are all gone now." "I must go" snapped Kanotchy, breaking Olena's train of thought. "You must catch up with your family so your father may find you." Casting his footwear aside, Kanotchy bounded over the rise, quickly rejoining the other braves.

Wagons, people, animals and guards continued all day, arriving at a hastily prepared site near the Southwest corner of Mansfield commons in a little ravine with a creek snaking through it. Exhausted, footsore, dusty and hungry, the Delaware made camp where they could, with what they had. Accommodations were cramped and poorly organized as only the hunters were accustomed to camping away from their homes. Militia guards offered little assistance.

Mansfield

Ravens cawed a mocking welcome as Levi Jones unlocked, then kicked open, the ill-fitting door at the rear of the trading post in Mansfield town after a long night of playing cards till dawn at the tavern. "This headache will be the death of me," Jones said aloud as he peered into the darkness. At the end of the long room, from behind the cooperage, John Chapman emerged through a doorway carrying a lantern and a loaf of fresh bread. He lit a candle from the lantern which he placed on a cracker barrel, then went about igniting wicks of oil lamps overhead. The growing light cast long shadows revealing two sleeping figures huddled together by the fireplace. "Dammit Johnny, I thought you was watching my shop, not running a boarding house!" chided Jones. Chapman smiled at the suffering shop keeper and handed him the bread. "Oh, don't mind them, just a few of my Native acquaintances sleeping-off the cider. Say, is there any more of that salted butter?"

Jones glared at his ragged friend from behind the counter. "I leave you here, alone, one night, and already the mice and cockroaches have to compete for living space with drunken savages! Does Colonel Kratzer know of this?"

Unaffected by the merchant's rant, Chapman yawned, and then replied: "The Colonel is a very busy man. These are not of the Greentown lot, if that's what you are afraid of. No sir, that there's Seneca John and Quilipetoxe, the Colonel's scouts, came back from Jeromestown last night."

"Then why aren't they bivouacked with the militia like they's supposed to?" snapped Jones, nudging the Indians to consciousness with the tip of his boot.

"They came here last night," recalled Chapman, turning his attention to the bread. "Seneca John said he has a debt to pay you—those hides near the door there. When I told them you went home for the night, they plum refused to leave. By-the-bye, Quilipetoxe told me he ran into that old Wyandot, Toby, on the Leesvillle road. He was carrying a sack of beeswax into town. When Quilipetoxe told Toby of the goings-on at Greentown, Toby bade him bring the beeswax to you and ran off into the woods. I put the sack up with the hams in the cold cellar." Jones shook his head and placed a jug of metheglyn and a mound of tobacco next to his ledgers. "Well, that meeting on the road probably saved old Toby's life. The Colonel issued orders to kill any redskin not under Douglass's guard. The order stands until the Greentown lot is removed from Mansfield."

"Bad for business I say." Jones paused, looking at the freshly skinned pelts on the floor. "No, we will lose more than just trade goods, John, it's a gut feeling."

"Well, it is a shameful thing, pitiable," added Chapman, moving away from Jones as the two braves staggered to the counter.

"Oh, I see you are still full of my liquor," sneered Jones, corking the jug. "But that's alright, being guests and all. Hope you slept well down there." Seneca John ignored the sarcasm, staring enviously at a row of leather hip boots lining the back wall.

"We have come to settle our debts and retrieve what is ours," said Quilipetoxe examining the merchant's tobacco. Jones removed the clay pipe from its place on the mantle and wiped down the bowl with his shirt sleeve. "Those hides you have will suffice, but I fear I cannot return those muskets you pawned last week. It would not go well for me if I was accused of arming Indians just now, you understand." In a flash of anger at this breach of agreement, Seneca John's fist hit the counter, shattering the pipe's clay stem and showering Jones with tobacco.

"Give us what is ours or we will take it," growled the seething warrior. Jones stepped backwards quickly unsheathing a cavalry pistol from an open saddlebag, pulling it to full cock with one easy motion.

"You will be taking nothing from me in this life

you Godless scum!" assured Jones, mortified.

"You can't shoot us both," Quilipetoxe stated flatly as he moved closer to Jones. "We have made good on our part. Now you break your word. Let us talk peacefully."

"Put down your gun," insisted Chapman as he interceded to defuse things. "Now Levi, hand me that pistol and pour yourself some coffee before you get someone killed. They are army scouts, loyal ones at that. Give them the muskets and be done with it."

"Loyalty?" scoffed Jones. "You'll tell me about loyalty as they tie me to the whipping post. If they are not loyal to their own kind, what's to stop them from putting a ball in my back?" With his free hand Jones wiped the sweat from his forehead using the hem of his apron. "You best get these cutthroats out of my gunsights before I pull the trigger."

Chapman felt humiliated and was tempted to walk out with the Indians, leaving Jones alone with his fears. Seneca John spat on the counter before storming out the door and Jones lowered his aim from the scout's back. Reaching for the jug, the shaken merchant took a pull, then another, finally putting down the loaded pistol.

"You can take those hides with ya," said Jones in a softer voice. "Don't let me or anyone else see you around my store again, ever again, do ya here?" Quilipetoxe plucked the bundle off the floor and left without saying a word. Jones sat down at his bench and looked up at the two muskets on the wall. "They've been bold as brass ever since Hull surrendered Detroit. I should never have done business with them devils." Chapman took the pistol and the jug and placed them on a high mantle at the far end of the room, then turned to Jones and said "I hope that's the end of it Levi; what did you ever get into?"

Toby, the Indian encountered by Quilipetoxe on the Leesville Road, had hurried to Mansfield when he heard the news from Greentown. There, from a safe distance, he observed and evaluated activities of the militia, who were assembling outside the square-hewn blockhouse—the smaller of two—posted on roads into the motley village. Ten militiamen led by a man Toby knew quite well were assembling for drill, having enjoyed a few drinks to fortify themselves against the late summer sun. They resembled farmers more than soldiers, lacking any sort of military discipline. Toby sat and watched, his face hidden by the brim of his tarpaulin hat. He could see nearby oxcarts and wagons in neat rows. They were piled high with jumbled belongings and were watched over by a skinny boy playing jacks.

Downrange, pumpkins were set atop ten stumps that studded the naked hillside. Toby waited for the first volley, moving only when the soldiers were busy reloading their muskets. John Gilkison began dressing-down his inept charges. "That was terrible," he shouted. "Why do I still see pumpkins? I want you all to take your knives and dig the lead out of that maple grove. Backwoods turnips!"

Drawing no attention, Toby approached and removed his hat. Gilkison took notice of his presence. There was an uncomfortable moment of hesitation before he extended a hand in salutation. "You are taking your life in your hands, old friend," said the sergeant with a look of consternation. "What is your business here?" Toby glanced away, suspecting the volunteers had seen him and were getting suspicious. He appraised various escape routes, but he had to get information.

"My daughter has been taken by your men and I do not know why. Can you help me, my brother?" Gilkison drew a deep breath and guided Toby, an elder from the Upper Sandusky village, away from the curious men who were awaiting further instructions.

"You know I cannot aid you, as much as it pains me to tell you so—breaks my heart. These soldiers are not fooling around. They are to kill anyone who escapes." Lost for words, Toby paced back and forth nervously touching a hideous battle scar that ran down his left cheek.

"Tell me brother, where do I find her?" he said at last. Gilkison stepped closer to the desperate Wyandot while keeping an eye on the Corporal who was drawing nearer.

"Listen to me, Toby. Your only hope is to lay low if you intend to leave Mansfield alive." With a loud cough, the Corporal interrupted, saluting Gilkison before speaking.

"The boys are ready for another volley, sir, at your ready." Gilkison looked the Corporal up and down as the young man hurriedly wiped tobacco juice from his breast plate and horn.

"Why are the lads out of formation?" snapped Gilkison. No matter, let us try to kill our pumpkins at twenty paces—now bugger off!" Toby stood still as his friend drilled through him with an urgent stare.

"Get the hell out of here!" he whispered. "Go north and stay there. You will be of no use to your daughter dead! I'm sorry I can't help you. My orders are to enforce Kratzer's directives and train these Johnathans for war," he admitted with a touch of guilt. Toby saluted his old friend in the corporeal fashion of the recruits, quickly while making his way through the gathering riflemen without being challenged. A few of the local volunteers laughed at the out-of-staters who still took the old familiar Indian for the sergeant's scout.

Gilkison had unwittingly revealed too much about the situation, Toby thought as he counted plumes of smoke rising from the direction of the tanning yard near Ritter's mill run east of town. Alone and unarmed, he selected a fallen bough from a nearby maple, broke it down until the piece matched the length of his forearm, a practical weapon in a scuffle, he thought. His eyes closed in a moment of concentration, trying not to remember the last time he was in a real fight, until the piercing howl of a dog shattered his meditation and sent him scrambling up the bank above the encampment.

Hungry cockerels scratched around the periphery of a cook wagon, kicking up kernels of parched corn from an old reed basket while a scullion honed a butcher's blade. In the center of camp, a small bleating goat hung from a branch near the fire, kicking pitiably as a scout hurriedly flayed it alive, much to the dismay of the captive Delaware camped there.

Nearly all the guards had left camp, moving toward the stench of the tannery grounds where two great bleeding dogs circled each other, baited by the volunteers. "This tops any card game or cockfight back home" mused Morrison to a nervous quartermaster. "I'll be able to buy a command with my winnings when the dust settles." A giant half-wolf named King George lunged onto the back of a great black guard dog taken from Armstrong's lodge the night before, his claws tearing downward into the black creature's legs with an audible crunch. Their jaws locked as the outmatched opponent buckled at the knees and tumbled to the ground. Morrison gleefully descended on the pair, easing a bayonet between their jaws and wrenching them apart. "By thunder, your dog's neck has been bitten through-and-through shouted Morrison to the quartermaster, pointing to black froth bubbling from the defeated beast's gaping mouth. Morrison grinned, passing a jug to his sulking opponent. "You best git rid of your dog before Douglass arrives. He has no stomach for sport. I'd better collect my winnings before the lads turn out. Keep that jug for your troubles. Next time steal a meaner dog!" McCullough carefully fit a muzzle of braided husk over the victor's snout and daubed yarrow powder into its deepest wounds.

Olena was cold, and the tannery pond's stench got to her stomach. She could not eat, instead passing the bowl to her ravenous cousin. Some had waded into the run to wash, exposing themselves to the taunts of ogling guards. Armstrong and his remaining council sat silently under a giant beech while an elderly woman removed an iron cook pot from a tiny fire, pouring sumac broth into the last of several canteens. Olena and Naomi busied themselves loading a small cart with what brushwood they could find, using it to conceal a heavy iron tripod which had miraculously not been stolen. Feeling melancholy and hopeless, Silas wandered around seeking something to do, quietly harnessing the remaining ponies, checking and rechecking every buckle, ring and knot. He felt sick. A position in council, his birthright, had been given him in haste along the trail to Mansfield. Titles had no more meaning, he thought, than a pretend rank bestowed on him by children. Sharing the labor with women made him especially vitriolic. The smaller girls were distracted by Naomi who was fashioning a doll from buckhorn stalks. Silas paused. Olena guessed what was coming next and backed away from her work.

"Have you no shame! All that we were has vanished before us," said Silas. The angry young man leaped forward seizing Naiomi by the wrist. "Go and play around your anguished parents." Silas released the terrified girl, pushing her aside.

Jim Jerk, a venerated elder, took notice, leaving his place under the ancient beech to quiet the Chieftain's ranting son. He led Silas away from the gathering Delaware and stopped under a long-dead oak. "Silas, you are part of a sacred trust. You must lead by example like your father." The young man lowered his head avoiding the elder's eyes.

"My father wishes himself dead and so do I. We are no better than herded sheep," Silas exclaimed without thinking.

"Your father does not let his anguish show. You will grow to do the same, but you will never be free of the careless words that you say today. Let us return to camp as we have been noticed by the soldiers who are not as sober as we."

Toby, who had been carefully observing the encampment, eased into the mill run downstream of a militiaman who was squatting over a makeshift latrine. In his youth he would have murdered the unwary man, or at least made-off with his rifle. Still, the gun, of Kentucky origin, hung unattended from a limb well out of the straining soldier's reach. Loud voices from the tree line ended Toby's temptation as he slipped into the shadows of some tall grass and squatted under the weathered roots of a blown-down maple.

Toby observed that discipline was lax as he counted ten or twelve militiamen taking shade under the mottled willows that encircled the camp following the outline of the bending stream. Near the center of the meadow, Armstrong's Delaware, several hundred in all, milled about restlessly giving the elders assembled under the great tree a wide berth. Toby strained to hear as the roughshod McCullough stepped within feet of his gnarly cage. "We'll have to march straight through the heat of the day if we wait here much longer," growled Morrison looking across the run. McCullough nodded in agreement as he spat out his chaw.

"You marched through much worse, Morrison. At least this time there ain't no war party on our heels, just these broken dogs," McCullough replied.

"We should pack 'em all into the tanner's shed and set 'em alight if you ask me," Morrison said, exposing a jaw line empty of teeth. "Hell, we'd be doin' the tanner a great favor. Escort duty my ass! We'd be well clear of Mansfield if it weren't for Captain Douglass and that Goddamn Gilkison taking half the men to a wedding." McCullough cut-off another plug and handed the twist to Morrison.

"I guess they needed an escort themselves," scoffed McCullough as he washed his hands in the creek. Fortunately, they did not stay long, leaving the bank for a water butt further down the ravine. Toby watched in frustration as they hoisted the barrel and moved off toward the camp's center. He stood up and squeezed into a dense matting of green river willows. The thought of hand-to-hand fighting both terrified and excited him, a sensation he could not shake. He emerged from the foliage carefully tucking his club into the folds of his blouse. Something was wrong. He turned around, bumping into a large scowling soldier. Toby recoiled slowly raising both hands.

"Put down your hands you lazy son-a-bitch!" croaked the militiaman as he shoved a bucket of water into his hands. "Shame on y'all making me and your womenfolk do all the damn work. Take this to the barrel at the head of the line." Toby nodded, then disappeared into the mulling mass of refugees. Much relieved, he moved to the head of the line where Silas sat on a gray pony. Toby's eyes moved from one head to another as he placed the bucket in a nearby wagon bed. Then he saw her—Olena's familiar profile sitting with the lading near the rear of the cart.

The girl looked ill, lurching forward as the restless oxen shifted on their tether. In back of him, Toby could hear John Gilkison's voice issuing orders from horseback. Gilkison concentrated the bulk of his forces at both ends of the line. Time was running out when the procession began to move forward.

Reaching the cart was no easy feat because the militiamen had packed Delaware and beasts alike tightly in a dusty line of conveyances, and displaced people. Toby whistled, then called her name, eliciting no response in the din and confusion. At the head of the train Silas's ears picked up and he rose in his saddle and brought his horse to a halt. Toby quickened his pace until he came alongside the pony.

"I grieve for your people, young Armstrong," said Toby above the shrill whistle of a soldier's fife. Silas looked away briefly from the elder Wyandot, untying the leather water skin from his saddle horn.

"You need not worry about it," Silas said flatly. He passed the skin to Toby. "Take your girl while you can still escape. I will distract any soldier who takes notice." Toby nodded in approval as Silas leaned over and plucked the tarpaulin hat from Toby's head. "This is a strange hat, elder." Toby shrugged his shoulders, wincing in the sunlight. "My daughter made it," he replied.

With a whoop Silas pushed his pony forward coming within sight of the chieftain's cart. With a snap of the wrist he let fly the hat which landed with a thud at Olena's feet. She recognized immediately what was happening and beamed with joy as her father hopped up on the open gate of the cart. Without hesitation, she threw her arms around Toby's neck and sobbed. After a moment he broke her grip and clutched her shoulders saying "Listen to me! Can you run?" Olena nodded and jumped off the wagon ahead of her father.

"I see no guards on either side of us," said Olena out loud. Toby gripped her arm tightly, pulling her forwards and hurting her. "What are we going to do now?" cried the girl, recoiling from her father's grip.

"We are going to shut our mouths; then we are going to run! Most of the soldiers are behind us and in front," whispered Toby. "Half of them are mounted. We will find the right time and terrain and then we'll run for our lives!"

Giant maples arched overhead like rows of sentries, their thick trunks scarred by marks from ancient sugar taps. A bright blue sky soon became lost under the forest's dim canopy. Toby and Olena quickened their pace as they ducked into a gap created by Silas's horse. "I am going to drop behind you. The soldiers will be watching me," said Armstrong over his shoulder. Olena felt her father's grasp tighten as he quickened the pace. "Are you ready?" asked Toby, his eyes trained on the surrounding tree line. "When you run, make the trees your shield and never show your back directly to the soldiers and their guns. I will follow." Olena kissed her father's hand and she leaped off of the trail. Silas snapped in the reins causing his horse to rear abruptly.

"What is Armstrong up to?" asked Douglass. His eyes narrowed as he caught sight of a leg disappearing behind a tree, exposing the ruse.

Muskets cracked from the head of the column, as gunsmoke obscured his view. "Damn it, McCullough, Morrison, let's bring them back!" shouted Gilkison, unsheathing his rifle.

Olena was a dancing fox, weaving in and out of the dense underbrush, her father close behind. McCullough ducked behind a chestnut, steadying his rifle on a low branch. Patiently he followed the pair with his sights, training his aim ahead of the girl. He exhaled and squeezed the trigger. Toby fell in a heap. The girl was nowhere to be seen. Gilkison was the first to reach the Dying Wyandot. He uncorked the stopper of his canteen and offered Toby some water which he swallowed as he put his hand on Gilkison's shoulder, struggling to speak. "My friend..."

"Damn you, I'll make a friend out of you," interrupted McCullough excitedly. Morrison drew his tomahawk and handed it to the wild-eyed McCullough, "Do it! Do it George. Take revenge for your brother's blood," snapped Morrison, pulling Toby from the brush.

"You have taken your revenge!" shouted Gilkison standing up. "You put a big damn hole in his chest."

"We get our orders from Kratzer," chided Morrison, "and so do you, Sergeant. Let's brain the dog and be done with it." With a crack, the top of Toby's head came off flooding the grass with spurts of blood. Gilkison winced and looked away.

"You will bury this man, McCullough, do you hear me? By God you will dig the grave!"

"Damn you," spat McCullough, severing the head. "They killed my brother and never buried him. I should take his heart for my supper," lamented Morrison as he rolled the corpse down a steep ravine into a creek bed.

In the weeds, concealed by ferns, Olena took her rest as hungry gnats swarmed about, burrowing into the corners of her eyelids. A sinking desperation came over her as she listened to the birds and frogs. They signaled her father's death with their return to normal behavior. It was also apparent that her pursuers had gone away. She would be utterly, inescapably alone in her flight to find her relatives at the Wyandot Village near Upper Sandusky.

Coffinberry House

Wild hogs, caked in filth from the market grounds, rummaged through refuse near the western edge of Mansfield village commons. Toby's butchered skull stood guard over the muck from its place atop the sharpened settlement mail post where it remained, impaled through the shattered cranium and an empty eye socket. As villagers took pains to avoid it, turkey vultures loitered around this grizzly meal baking in the sun, sticky and stinking and now the domain of bottle flies and hornets.

"Just disgraceful," griped Mrs. Winship as she stepped over a full spittoon in the doorway of Williams tavern, and pushed her way through the unwashed soldiery. Young Sarah Gilkison was not far behind, leaving her baby in the arms of the busy tavern keeper. Startled toughs and rowdies cleared a path for her, some politely removing their hats. Brisk and crisp Mrs. Winship charged a great table near the hearth where Colonel Kratzer held court. A glare from the venerable seamstress ended bawdy table talk and brought the scowling Colonel's face up from his paperwork.

"Well, Mrs. Winship, what fresh complaints do you have for me today," sneered the Colonel. "Let me guess—your husband lost his breeches at the card table again and now you want them back!" The crowd erupted with laughter, noticeably reddening Mrs. Winship's face and causing her eyes to squint as she snapped, "You know why I'm here!" Her arm and index finger pointed at the mail post. "What manner of savage are you Colonel?"

"The kind that does not like interruptions," replied Kratzer, picking his teeth.

Sarah Gilkison stepped forward and put a comforting hand on Mrs. Winship's shoulder. "Begging your pardon, Colonel," she said softly. "This is not the Tower of London after all. We are not used to such brutal practices." Kratzer smiled and poured himself a drink. "Ah yes, pretty Sarah Gilkison, the Sergeant's wife, is it? Well now, let us hope you are not speaking on behalf of your husband, eh? I suggest you go home before I summon him to explain your behavior. It was, after all, your husband's men who made such an example of that poor old wretch. You should ask him about it! And you, Mrs. Winship, your husband is the postmaster of this louse town, is he not? The mail post bearing the head in question is his responsibility—think on that!"

"It is savagery!" interrupted Mrs. Winship angrily.

"It is good for the morale of my men," retorted Kratzer finishing his dram. "My dear Mrs. Winship, we are slowly losing this war to the common Indian. The bulk of my men—boys really––have never fired a volley in anger, but they have all heard tales of murder, rape and worse at the hands of savages who they know by name. Who know them by name! Neighbors so to speak. My men feel powerless, you understand, and they fear for their loved ones back home. If putting a head on a pole from time-to-time quenches anxieties, then so be it."

"We shall gather a petition," snapped Mrs. Winship, as if martialing the forces of heaven as she turned for the door. Kratzer poured another drink and without looking up from the bottle said, "Do not think me unfeeling, Mrs. Winship. If you want that head down, you may remove it yourself. I suggest you plant it in your garden come Spring." Hoots of laughter spread around the table, depriving Mrs. Winship of any further retort. Mrs. Gilkison left her side, vanishing with her child into the smoke and shadows of the dimly lit tavern.

Sergeant Gilkison and Levi Jones stood in front of the Coffinberry house which sat proudly atop the far side of Mansfield commons, impervious to buffeting winds that whistled through poorly daubed walls of neighboring dwellings. At the far end of the yard, George Coffinberry huddled over a small brass cannon, fussing with its elevation. A gun crew stood with their backs to the wind, impatient with Coffinberry's tinkerings. It was not the first time this village elder had held things up, now insisting they drill in accordance with a manual he had found stuffed in the gun's short barrel.

"It's just a pop-gun," shouted Gilkison from the relative warmth of Coffinberry's doorway. "Sounds like a big 12 pounder, though—probably a signal gun." Levi Jones glared back, plugging his ears with both hands. "George is proud of its report," continued Gilkison at the top of his lungs. "He named the toy 'old bunty'."

"This is some kind of hell, John, is it not," growled Jones, cutting the Sergeant off. "That rum pot Governor and Kratzer have all but shut down trade in this county, by Christ, and I thought the savages were the problem?" Without comment, Gilkison invited Jones into the front room of his in-law's cabin. It was not like the rude lean-tos scattered around the square, or the squat dwellings of Mount Vernon, but a spacious, if not stately home of two stories. The ground floor was built of logs, square hewn, with dovetailed corners. Its upper story, plastered and painted, reflected the styles of German Pennsylvania. Mrs. Coffinberry sat at the spinning wheel, rhythmically working the

treadle as if in a trance, pausing only to change out the bobbin. Jones did not bother her, stepping gingerly around a great pile of wool and into the kitchen where Gilkison had disappeared. "I heard you disarmed a couple of scouts in your store a few days back," chided Gilkison as he lifted the lid off of a stew pot near the hearth. "From what I understand they took the complaint straight to Kratzer, who ordered them back on patrol without their muskets and kit. When they didn't turn out at reveille, Kratzer ordered them shot on sight if discovered. Jones accepted a plate from Gilkison and found a stool to sit on.

"I'm afraid you've run up quite a bill this month," said Jones, quickly changing the subject. He launched into the hot stew. "Two pounds of lead, three jugs of rye, and special gum ink brought up by my cousin from Cincinnati at great personal risk. There aren't enough literate people in this town to support your printing press let alone read your papers." He leaned in toward Gilkison and looked him sternly in the eye. "I don't mean to pry, John, but when will you remove your trophy from its perch on the square? It's bad business, you know. How am I supposed to pay your father-in-law his rent? Believe me when I say I am no friend of the Indian, but Toby, you understand, was no Tecumseh. The local women were quite fond of the old man and his medicinals."

"I could not save him," replied Gilkison sharply. "I took no part or pleasure in this exhibition. By God it haunts me! He was condemned to death the moment he sprinted off the trail." The spinning wheel slowed to a stop, bringing the prickly subject to a welcome end. Jones looked around the room as if to find a new topic. Gilkison's small type-press sat in the kitchen corner, taking up precious space. Mrs. Coffinberry had long since made use of it as a coat rack and bonnet stand. An assortment of weaponry lined the wall, ready at a moment's notice, giving the kitchen a fortress-like feel. Jones took another look at the press as he sank his bowl in a bucket of murky dishwater.

"That press will yield more punch than volley will," said Gilkison ending the silence.

"Spare me," replied Jones. "You should have sold it to the blacksmith for scrap while he still had coin. By the time you ink that thing up and get it running, reading will have gone out of fashion." Jones stood up and brushed the crumbs from his homespun vest. "Newsprint, though valuable on the shithouse bench, sure offers little protection against Indians, or redcoats, or thieves, or wolves for that matter. No sir, I place my faith in powder from my horn."

Gilkison made his way to the door and pried two silver coins from a hiding place behind the molding. "This year has brought us dampness and sick wheat," he said bitterly. "Right now, agriculture is as uncertain as commerce. Your ambitions remain as precarious as my own. Indians and redcoats are the least of your problems. I suggest you hold on to this sum; keep it under your hat."

Odyssey

Maple seeds fell like snowflakes, twirling their way to the dank ground. The narrow trail, long used by animals, broadened, its familiar obstacles opening into a vast constricting swamp. Olena kneeled in the fetid sludge trying to liberate her moccasins from its tightening grip, but they were lost as she stumbled back to her feet. Thickets of distant swaying reeds, backlit by the setting sun, glowed like the mantle of a lamp. Olena, suddenly engulfed by a cloud of ravenous mosquitoes, threw off her dress, and furiously slapped the black-gray ooze all over her body, soon sealing out her bloodthirsty tormentors.

Bleached and rotting snags of a long dead forest dotted the landscape and provided refuge for nesting birds, and their predators. Realizing the need to prepare for nightfall, Olena bundled as many dry reeds as she could carry and stuffed them into the hollow crotch of a barren tree high above the living swamp. She selected a stout stick to use as a weapon if unwelcome visitors tried to approach her nest. There was no sleep the first few hours of darkness as her mind unraveled a tangle of painful events that brought her to this foreboding place. Olena had heard shots, but had not seen her father fall, just the blur of passing trees as she ran for her life. She tried not to think of the ferocity wrought upon him in his final moments, or the constant desperation of being hunted. Sometimes she would imagine herself in her father's form, helpless to prevent the tomahawk's bite, but the howl of a wolf would return her attention to the here-and-now.

The mire, a dormant monster, harbored a legion of glowing eyes, which reflected light from the waxing moon, and grew more malevolent with each passing hour. Eventually, a curtain of fog wound its way across the reed beds and snaked up the trees, swallowing Olena in an ethereal mist. Her eyelids slowly closed knowing the great beast had vanished, taking with it the horror of the night.

When she awoke there was no sun, its nurturing warmth lost in the pervasiveness of the damp morning mist. Olena clambered down the base of the tree and seized a long cane which she planted firmly in the muck of an open spot. She waited. Her father had instilled in her the importance of determining distance, direction and time. She remembered the old compass Toby carried in the folds of his knapsack, a treasure lifted from the corpse of a royal surveyor when he was a child. Its mysterious pointer always indicated North whether the sun shone or not, confirming her belief in the spirit realm. Soon a long finger-like shadow spread from the cane westward, then disappeared again. She had no doubt this was the shadow of her father's hand pointing the way home.

A large snapping turtle watched over his domain from the dry end of a submerged log amidst hundreds of schooling gizzard shad, herded into a swirling column by two giant basking gar. "I must be near the great Sandusky," said Olena out loud as she observed the enormous river fish. A wounded shad struggled to the surface, its air bladder bulging through an open hole behind the gill cover. Most living things can be eaten raw she recalled as she eviscerated the struggling fish with the tip of her knife. She scraped loose its pungent entrails, held her breath and forced down the unsavory flesh and liver, leaving the offal for turtles to devour. Olena looked up at the clearing sky. The light had strengthened, illuminating golden crests of grassy hummocks which rose above the water like stepping stones toward a distant tree line.

Crossing the vast swamp had taken up much of the afternoon, it's saw grass and hidden obstacles rubbing raw patches of unprotected skin. Olena collapsed in a heap below the forest's ridge line, and was racked by violent cramps pulsing through her calves, the result of dragging her feet through the tangle. An intermittent stream of clear water slowly trickled from a crack above the bank and collected in a small pocket deep within a fissure in the weathered rock. Standing on tip toes, she tried to get her hand to the water, but to no avail. She needed the clean clear water and was determined to get at it. She removed the medicine bag from around her neck, carefully placed its contents on a rock and removed the braided lanyard. She inserted one end into the gap and dressed the other over the rock and into her watertight bag. Soon the lanyard was damp and then dripping as drops collected one-by-one. Now all she needed to do was wait. She welcomed the chance to pause and regain her strength. Once rested, she drank the cool water from her bag, climbed to its source on the ridge and drank her fill. There was a trail of sorts, which small animals had cut deep into the foliage until it disappeared underneath a blackberry thicket. While keeping out of sight, Olena gorged herself on the largest berries.

The sudden roar of gunfire jarred her from her feast and sent a thousand passenger pigeons aloft, momentarily darkening the sky. A wounded doe crashed through a nearby thicket and disappeared over a steep river bank. Hunters drew closer guided by a bloody trail that shimmered down a wall of thorns. "I can't see no deer," muttered one of the men as he scaled a tree for a better view. The other hunter leaned into the thicket plucking a blood-soaked leaf from its trampled stalk. He tasted it. "There's bile in the blood," he said as he spat out the leaf. Olena closed her eyes as the roughshod man waded deeper into the tangle, so close she could smell him. She held her breath and mentally became one with the forest floor. "That deer's gut shot," he shouted to his partner. "I ain't going through this whole damn thicket for tainted meat—probably down in the Sandusky anyhow."

"There's always pigeon," complained his partner. Both men quickly disappeared allowing Olena a slow retreat to the familiar river willows and twisted snags that covered a wide flood plain. She recognized this plain as the one which, upstream a ways, skirted the western edge of her village. She had found her way home.

In the days that followed, Olena reunited with her grandmother who nursed her cuts and bruises, while schooling her intensively on the formalities and traditions expected of her inside the council house. The thought of being interrogated about her ordeal made her nauseous, and indeed she incurred Grandma's anger when she became ill in-route to council.

Olena sat silent before the council fire, glancing around the many elders packed together on the longhouse floor. Smoke and the rank odor of bruin fat mingled with the fresh air from an open window, its draft helping little to freshen the sweating audience.

"Will we give battle?" shouted an angry voice from the back of the hall. It was Kanotchy, who with a band of followers had fled Greentown the day of the evacuation and were now renegades. He looked down at his pipe, tamping the bowl with his calloused thumb. "No, we will go south and burn their farms. Let the soldiers fear for their children and wives. Let us trade sorrow for sorrow."

"No good will come of it," interrupted the elder Philipus who rose to address the council as a

Wyandot leader. "The more we kill, the smaller our world becomes. Their numbers grow, occupying the houses of those we have vanquished. I am growing old. I have slaughtered white men until my arms were tired from the work, and yet have reaped nothing from it. My arms are still tired and I do not wish to awaken the beast who sleeps on our doorstep."

The council muttered in agreement, ignoring the rhetoric of Kanotchy's followers. Philipus looked Kanotchy in the eye. "Fill your stomachs and leave this place. I will not bring Armstrong's fate upon us. You are a danger to all, including yourself. Go to Piqua and build a cabin. Farm whatever land they give you. Olena is without a father. Why not take her as your wife?"

"Perhaps you are right," said Kanotchy, staring into the flames. "I no longer enjoy the thought of war. We will leave you in peace to decide our fate among ourselves."

Philipus took a long draw from the pipe, passed it with reverence to the holy man in the shadows and then turned his attention to the door through which he could see his elderly wife snapping beans. "Think hard upon it brother, as you no longer have Tecumseh's ear."

"I will leave it in the hands of my people," replied Kanotchy as he ran his fingers over Olena's neck. "Do not worry. Your father will be avenged, in this life or the next." She turned away in disgust and stormed through the door.

Outside the council house, a majestic old stag had been slaughtered, its head and entrails suspended in the forks of a long bough mounted to the roof. From the fields a lengthy procession of chanting women made their way to the river to bathe while men danced before the harvest table.

"I hope he never returns," said Olena to Philipus's wife as they washed themselves in the Sandusky. The thought of his caress ashamed her and yet awakened in her a feeling she could not share with the elder's wife.

"Do not dwell upon it," said the matriarch as she wrung the water from her hair. "Kanotchy is a dead man, he all but deemed it so in the longhouse. He will never return."

At dawn Olena hurried back to the river where her grandmother stood on the bank holding an angry catfish by the gills. At her feet was the damaged trap which had captured the beast. Olena sat and wove a willow branch through the fish's gills, holding the ends tightly as grandmother drew the skin away with her knife. With one sharp snap, the head and entrails separated from the still writhing fish. She leaned against a tree and mended the shattered trap while Olena occupied herself by rolling strips of dogbane between her palms and adding it to the length of twine forming around her wrist.

"I couldn't trap a fish or make twine when I was your age," said grandmother as she reflected on her childhood. "I had to learn fast after I was taken from my family's camp. You must always be resourceful; always be aware." She inspected the mended fish trap one last time before adding the entrails and a large blue stone to the bottom, then sinking it below a riffle. "Your father, my son, had taken this advice to heart. That is why you are here with me now, my granddaughter. I can see my son's likeness deep within your eyes."

Olena broke eye contact with her grandmother. "I fear I will never see father again," she stammered.

"Do not bother your mind with fear," replied the matriarch placing her hands on Olena's shoulders. "If he does not find his way home it is because he hunts with his ancestors and is content."

Levi Jones

August, 1812

Boots dried by the warmth of hearth fires as shutters banged closed and rain lashed down in torrents. Mired alleyways and roads were soon abandoned to the pigs and geese, which were perfectly content scavenging in the rising filth. On Sturges corner, Levi Jones closed his shop and pulled his cloak tight around his shoulders as he began the journey home, wet and uncomfortable, taking no notice of the strangers who shadowed him from the wilderness that skirted the town.

Seneca John and Quilipetoxe kept a careful watch on Jones as the shop-keeper hurried out of view of the Mansfield Stockade. Quilipetoxe nervously ran his thumb down the blade of his skinning knife and watched as his friend took cover in underbrush across the road. Moments later Levi was startled from his thoughts when Seneca John  stepped behind him and plunged his knife all the way in. In a flash of rage, Quilipetoxe and Seneca John straddled their prey, stabbing him until their knives became too slippery to handle.

Wiping the knife handles, they went to work on the corpse, then stumbled off, disappearing into the surrounding wilderness, carrying Jones's scalp, as blood pooled over their muddy footprints.

Discovery of the body caused a sensation. There were fears of Indian uprisings and massacres fueled by Kanotchy's nearby activities. Even Chapman, who feared for Jones because of his encounter with Quilipetoxe and Seneca John, was taken in.

Two weeks later at Williams tavern in town, tinder sputtered then ignited as a silhouetted figure prodded coals beneath the cordwood. He spat into the hearth before returning to his bench with a lantern. An undulating candle flame cast dramatic lines across the patrons' faces, contorting the expressions of all in the room.

Heat rising from close-packed men and dense smoke from their pipes only added to the choking atmosphere that had been worsening all evening. Since Jones's murder, alarm had spread through the countryside. John Chapman ran on foot to Mount Vernon where he arranged for reinforcements from the military garrison at Coshocton. The troops had arrived, but there was a new incident involving the murder of the Zimmer family by Indians. Pappy Wilkeson leaned across a table, opening the lantern to light a taper for his pipe. "I was at the Zimmer place after the fight. You woulda thought it was a packing house. We buried Henry Zimmer and Ruffner, not knowing which was which." After a pause to light his pipe, he continued. "Christ, we found Kate near the fire with her brains in a mushpot." The barkeep glared at Wilkeson, putting an end to the revolting image. But it was no use. Around the table fear spread as two men who found the corpse of Levi Jones retold the story of their discovery to an increasingly anxious and drunken crowd. "The body was that of Levi Jones to be sure," said Haney Westphal. "I could recognize him from his boots."

Heat, hysteria and drunkenness were all progressing with the evening when Seneca John and Quilipetoxe happened into the room and, clueless as to what was taking place, advanced to the bar.

Williams pulled the stopper on a large jug, staring directly into their eyes. "You best leave

while you still have scalps on, I don't need any more problems." Seneca John opened the pouch around his neck, took out a silver coin and slid it across the counter to the worried barkeep, who took it. He leaned into John saying: "Look you, that buys a whole lot of trouble. If you know what is good for you..." Quilipetoxe stood up, grabbed Williams by the collar, throwing him off balance, and replied, "You think we are women? Give us our whiskey and you will have no trouble." Seneca John grabbed the jug from the proprietor and took a long pull before passing it to his nervous companion.

Haney Westphal pushed his cup aside and made his way to the strangers, stopping at intervals to regain his balance before seating himself by Seneca John.

"Well now, that's a very fine hat for a savage. I seem to remember a certain shop-keep owning a hat just like it," he proclaimed loudly. Seneca John ignored the not-so-veiled accusation, turning his back to Westphal, and taking another swig from the jug.

Haney pushed it further, "Of course you wouldn't know what I'm talking about, would you?" he sneered as he spat on the floor just missing the toe of John's boot. As Westphal continued to antagonize the Indians, a mob began assembling at a nearby livery, deciding the fate of the two assassins.

"That's enough badgering tonight Haney," bellowed Pappy as he pushed his way towards his neighbor, easing an arm underneath his shoulder and slowly helping him to his feet.

"What you need is fresh air and sleep. Maybe some of the wife's coffee," insisted Wilkeson, parking Westphal in the doorway while he sought the privacy of a nearby tree. Pappy took a deep breath as he unbuttoned his pants to take a leak. "Captain Douglass has been chasing Levi's assassins all week—maybe a dozen or more Indians—most likely the same-uns that killed the Zimmers. No sir, those two are not your Indians, hat or no hat."

"They are all Devils in my book, makes no difference to me." proclaimed Westphal.

Pappy emerged from the shadows scratching his backside before letting out a yawn. "They are our neighbors in this wilderness, like it or not. All the militia did was stir up a hornet's nest, burning Greentown and all."

"Neighbors?" sniffed Westphal. "Sounds like you've been drinking from Johnny Chapman's cup again." A loud crash followed by shouting brought Westphal outside the tavern as a half-crazed mob burst through the entrance, knocking him on his back as the crowd threw the Indians into the street. Isaak Williams was last out the door. He bent over to lend Westphal a hand. The three men stood on the porch watching Seneca John and Quilipetoxe retreat out of town, the crowd hurling insults and rocks. As the twosome stumbled homeward through the mud, they were followed by several men armed with rifles and knives.

Plaintive cries of howling wolves and the sound of snapping branches alerted Quilipetoxe as he scanned the dimly moonlit hillside for any sign of Seneca John. They had become separated during the desperate scramble to get clear of their pursuers. His wounded head was beating painfully, like the slow rhythm of a drum, when the wafting stench of bear grease directed him towards a spring. There he spied his friend lying next to a rock drinking the runoff. Cupping his hands to his mouth, Quilipetoxe mimicked the call of a Mourning Dove. Seneca John rolled over and replied. The two hunkered down in a ravine as darkness enveloped them.

 Quilipetoxe exchanged the last of his jerky for a small amount of bear grease which he applied liberally, warding off the pestilence of mosquitoes and gnats that tormented him. The call of wolves, which grew steadily louder, was soon answered by the baying of hounds. Alarmed, Seneca John tossed his jerky aside and scrambled up the ravine, disappearing into the adjacent wetlands. Now alone, Quilipetoxe headed for the Black Fork River in a mad crawl that left him flailed raw by blackberry canes.

From across the swamp forest, sudden musket fire momentarily illuminated the tree tops, closely followed by the sharp reports, then by the chuckle of far-off voices. Quilepetoxe lay in the button bush, still as death, moving again only when the normal sounds of nature returned. The acrid smell of gunpowder provided a scent trail to the river, where an ominous scene of struggle revealed itself in the faint light. There, Quilipetoxe removed his friend's tomahawk from the mud before donning the fine hat lying beside it, the brim soiled with the blood of two murdered men.

Along one side of the bank, animals had established a well-beaten path to the meadow above, the same path he and Seneca John had used nearly a month earlier to ambush Levi Jones. All seemed momentarily tranquil as Quilepetoxe listened to the usual sounds of the meadow. A rabbit darted across the trail as an owl called from a nearby tree. Forest sounds seemed normal, but a trap was about to be sprung like the leap of a jumping spider.

A sudden jolt, of murderous intensity, spun Quilipetoxe backwards and into the brush. He instinctively tore his blouse in half clutching his abdomen as a second ball whistled past splitting a nearby sumac. He stifled the urge to vomit, biting down on one hand while opening the leaking wound with the other, confirming his worst fears.

"Did ya see that shot? Did ya see that!" echoed McCullough from the tree line. The vigilante slung his rifle over his shoulder, expertly shifting his weight on a branch high overhead.

"You probably hit them bushes, I can't hardly see a thing," rasped Morrison from below.

"I got 'em all right. I can smell the bastard," chuckled the hunter as he clambered down the tree.

The two men waded silently into the undergrowth, disappearing in the tall grass, knife and tomahawk in hand. The metallic stench of blood permeated the still air, beckoning them to the thicket where Quilipetoxe lay.

"Whoa, there you are, goddam you got 'em good." Near death, Quilipetoxe raised a hand in defense as a knife went to work on his scalp, scraping the crown of his skull. Then, with three sharp tugs, the trophy tore free. The two men stood over the dead Indian sharing a twist of tobacco.

"I wonder if the dogs have finished with the other savage."

"Hope they are still hungry." The thought of this spectacle made McCullough wince as he pulled Jones's top hat out of a blackberry bush and passed it to his partner.

As morning dawned on their camp, bacon sputtered and popped, crisping in a skillet suspended over hot coals. A young man busied himself pulverizing roasted chicory root with the butt of a rifle. Two scalps hung from the peak of a tripod slung over the fire, slow curing in the wisps of smoke. Near the camp a deep pit encircled hungry dogs as two lifeless bodies were buried. The men soon disbanded leaving Seneca John and Quilipetoxe to rest near the swamp East of the Mansfield settlement.

Beam's Mill

John Laylan waited impatiently in the cramped back room of Michael Beam's mill, among the whiskey barrels and joints of curing beef. A cool breeze wafted around the edges of a small greased paper window, venting the space of its rancidness. Still, it was little wonder Captain Martin preferred this place to the cave-like dampness of the blockhouse, or the endless complaints from locals in the tavern hall.

Laylan's thoughts drifted momentarily from his family in Mount Vernon to the crisp goose the barkeep's wife was pulling free of its skewer. "The Captain will be in shortly," sniffed Mrs. Beam, handing Laylan the parson's nose. "Eat quickly, Martin does not share victuals with petitioners. A brute of a bastard he is!" Laylan smiled as he savored his tiny but prized morsel.

The Reverend Copus sat next to him angrily peeling a gnarly green apple. "This is intolerable. Am I a prisoner here?" growled the Reverend, putting away his knife. "Staying here is costing me a small fortune. You cannot sleep in the blockhouse loft; it is occupied by dozens of angry hornets."

"You are lucky," said Laylan uneasily. "Your wife and kids are safe here. Evict the hornets and wait this out—for their sakes."

"If I don't get home and harvest, we will starve this winter," continued Copus softly. "I may be a country preacher, but I've been in scrapes before. We shouldn't worry so much. The Indians are busy preparing their tables for the green corn festival. For a week, you can be sure they will bear no grudges and create no mischief. I shall make the most of this peace, God be willing."

"The other night I was visiting my sister in Mansfield when I saw a couple of men drinking spirits in a cup fashioned from poor old Toby's scalp," interrupted Mrs. Beam in a hushed macabre voice. "When Kratzer stuck Toby's skull atop the mail post, my sister sent her daughter off to mother's house in Clinton until it is removed. You know, that swine says it is good for the morale of his men—the thought!"

"Were you in the Navy, Mr. Laylan?" asked Mrs. Beam, looking over his oilskin jacket. The plump millwright's wife squeezed past Reverend Copus and placed an apple in Laylan's coat pocket. "No Ma'am, just a merchantman's Jack turned soldier. Thank God I'm not in the Navy." Mrs. Beam pressed herself against his shoulder and almost whispered "There has been talk—Oh how I hate to gossip—that the British have built a squadron of frigates up on our lake, or so I've been told."

Laylan smiled. "They haven't the shipyards to build frigates, just small craft—brigs and such. I did get a taste of the British Navy, though. Not three months ago we were overtaken by a royal sloop of war near the Maumee. We hove-to, alarming a couple of Irish deserters we had working the deck. They plead with our Captain that they should surely hang if we did not fight it out. The lads and I would just as soon have pitched them into the lake than face a broadside." Laylan cleared his throat and continued. "Our Captain had the deserters taken below to the cabin of a passenger and neighbor of mine, Henry Levering, who was bedridden with dysentery. The Captain insisted these men hide in Henry's mattress while Henry lay atop of them. The boarding party from the sloop went below and ransacked the hold, stealing anything they fancied, while the sloop's officer examined the passenger manifest. Without even requesting a key to the door, one of them handed his mate a boarding ax and with three swings, the door crashed inward, knocking over a large chamber pot by the companionway. Well, the cabin floor was awash in filth and no one entered to question the sick man, lest they get shit on their boot heels."

Mrs. Beam blushed, covering her mouth with her apron. "You mean to say, Mr. Laylan, that a pot of dung saved your lives?"

"No ma'am," said Laylan, the smile returning to his face. "There is nothing more revolting to an officer's gentility than to carry a foul smell into his Captain's ward room—that's the truth. No, it was Levering who deserves most of the credit." Mrs. Beam chuckled to herself and was heard to say as she left the room, "Your lives were not in his hands, but under his arse!" Copus, his patience stretched to the limit, let out an embarrassed sigh, casting a sour glance to her backside as the door swung closed behind her.

The plank door swung open again with a wrenching groan. It smacked hard against Copus's knee as Captain Martin ducked through the opening and made his way into the crowded store room, placing his Razer hat on the cluttered bench top. "Have you been waiting long, Reverend?" he inquired.

"Interminably, yes," came the reply from Copus as he dug for his pipe. Martin turned his

attention to the goose, examining the platter like a surgeon.

"I've paid too much for this bird, alas! No tail." Martin poured a dram of rye waving

Mrs. Williams out.

"I did not come here to watch you eat dinner," groused Copus, laying down his tobacco pouch.

"Then how may I help you, Reverend," Martin inquired testily. "Ah yes, you wish to leave us. I cannot stop you, of course. But the wilderness, as you know is rife with savages, killers."

Copus's eyes narrowed. "Captain Douglass all but signed my death warrant when Greentown burned. Henry Zimmer and his wife are dead, along with Ruffner. Toby's head hangs over us all, atop the whipping post, thanks to their savagery."

"I need not be reminded in such a fashion! Not by a simple country parson," barked the Colonel, tossing his cup aside. "You may leave the blockhouse at your own peril—makes no difference to me."

Copus glared at Martin, "Will I receive an escort?"

"I can only spare a few men at most," replied the Captain with no trace of guilt. Copus nodded in approval and disappeared into the crowded hall.

Martin muttered to himself as he dipped his hands into a great clay washbasin below the window. He gazed at the abstract glow of the greased paper like a mystic seeing into the future. Then he noticed Laylan who had been silent. "What do you want from me?" asked Martin, returning from his thoughts. Laylan approached the table clutching his hat tightly with both hands. "I have come to make my plea for an early discharge."

Martin raised an eyebrow as Laylan continued. "With all respect, sir, Colonel Enos has stripped Mount Vernon of its men, leaving our women and young'uns to fend for themselves."

There was no reply as Martin studied him. Laylan was tall and sinewy with a shock of red hair tarred and plaited in a mariner's fashion. "You were a sailor, I see. What brought you to this militia?" asked Martin, pulling a wing from the platter.

"I had shipped aboard a grain schooner out of Cuyahoga. We were stopped by an armed brig with Colonel Enos as a passenger. He announced Hull's surrender of Detroit and the war declaration, urging us to pay off and join the militia. When we made port, hostilities with the redskins had broken out in Sandusky, so I moved my family inland and joined the first outfit I came across."

Growing impatient, Martin interrupted. "What about your concerns in Mount Vernon?"

"My brother-in-law was looking after the family in my absence. but the day before yesterday I happened upon him coming up Beal's Trail with Enos's militia. Their blacksmith told me they were at pains to leave, seeing as the violence has spread south."

Martin interrupted again. "I cannot discharge you. You have committed no crime, you are strong and healthy, a rarity in the militia. No, I cannot drum you out. But...I will grant you five days furlough." Martin placed his kerchief over the goose and pushed the plate aside. He turned and gave Laylan his full attention. "You settled your family in my neck of the woods. I can appreciate your fears. Tell me, your musket, do you own it?"

Laylan hesitated then replied, "No sir. I left my rifle with my wife. It was all she had until her brother arrived."

Martin waived him off. "I wish you had lied to me, Laylan. I would have lied to you. This is a patchwork army, threadbare. Some of the men shoulder squirrel guns. No sir, I cannot spare you that musket for your leave. We have purchased all the arms that could be had. Heed my advice and travel at night. Take the military road, no shortcuts. Never take that hat off. Gingered scalps are highly prized by savages."

Laylan removed his horn and munitions sack, placing them at the foot of the musket. He stepped through the door proclaiming, "I guess I'll travel unarmed like Chapman. Hell, if he can do it, I can do it.

Martin laughed, clapping his hands. "The savages leave Chapman alone because they think he's a madman. So do I! If you wish to be like Chapman you should shed your clothes, for an old flour sack over there and preach to the ticks and mosquitoes, Ha!"

Copus

Two iron cauldrons hung above a great mound of crackling embers. A beckoning aroma of venison and parsnips from the smaller one filled the lowlands. Fragrant apple butter simmered and thickened and turned brown in the other kettle, requiring constant stirring with a wooden scraper to prevent burning as it caramelized. Amy Copus watched with concern as her husband navigated the dodgy cabin roof until he found a beam to sit on. Raising a spyglass and muttering inaudibly, he surveyed the property from ridgeline to fields, searching for hidden dangers. "My husband is not himself today and it worries me," she admitted to Chapman with a touch of apprehension. "Last night he seemed so adamant that all would be well, yet he keeps his eyes on our fields as if the cornstalks are hiding assassins."

"I have noticed as much," said Chapman as he accepted a paw-paw from Copus's youngest daughter. "This morning I found him up a tree with that glass, auguring the tree line and field edges like a hawk. I told him that the lack of crows in the fields is a Godsend, not an evil omen." He took a bite then continued. "I've never known him to sulk away from a get-together, especially your cooking, Mrs. Copus."

She frowned and handed him the paddle. "Of course, the last time we made apple butter the

Armstrongs were our guests. Now he fears them. Do you think Armstrong killed the Zimmers?"

Chapman looked up at Copus on the roof and said: "It would shake my faith in mankind if that were so."

George Dye, a soldier from the escort, growled like a bear, contorting his face as if possessed. Henry and Wesley Copus circled the beast, snickering at the volunteer's wild impression. Young Nancy turned away, preferring to watch the handsome boy chop wood, a chore he took on without asking, after finishing supper. Other men lounged about near the big spring, gorging themselves on paw-paws, enjoying their leave time.

A bonfire had been kindled and the soldiers began once more to drink. John Tedrick tuned his fiddle as best he could amidst the cheers of those drawn to an impromptu wrestling match. John Chapman had left before nightfall, draped in a quilt from the family chest. The Reverend sat unhappily next to Tedrick, examining the crude fiddle bow his guest had fashioned from a chestnut branch that morning. "I feel as though we are being watched, Mr. Tedrick. Perhaps the men should bunk down in the cabin tonight," muttered Copus as he separated the horse hair with his fingertips. Tedrick rolled his eyes, snatching the bow from the Reverend's grip. "I just don't see the threat. You said yourself the Indians are on leave. I have not seen, nor for that matter smelled one for days. Perhaps you should get some shut-eye, take advantage of the peace while we still have it." Secretly Tedrick wanted to avoid having to sleep in the cabin with women and children, where they would have to act civilized and avoid partying with their mates on leave.

"The lads and I will sleep in the barn tonight, Reverend," interrupted Dye, who reached over to Tedrick for a pinch of tobacco. "We plan to whoop it up a little. You understand I'm sure. We are a bit well-oiled and wouldn't want to disturb your younguns."

Copus did not sleep well, disturbed by intermittent growls of the family dog. His thoughts grew less restrained, bringing back the memory of peeking through the door of Zimmer's cabin and slipping in the blood where wolves had begun to feast on the butchered occupants. George Launtze, the oldest of the volunteers, elected to stay with the Copuses, tempted by the promise of a straw mattress for his aching back. Launtze, a burly Prussian, had settled in a village neighboring Copus's birthplace and spent much of the evening distracting him with gossip from home. But as the night deepened, he fell asleep by the door, oblivious to the hungry mice chewing away at his dinner scraps, or to the troubled sheep that pushed against the sides of their pens outside. Behavior of the sheep, his dogs, and even the silence of the owls pervaded the night with warnings of forces unseen. Copus closed his eyes to pray, but his thoughts transported him to Greentown where he stood before the great council. God, he feared, had abandoned him when Greentown was put to the torch.

Morning dawned with the smell of bacon and Johnnycakes. Groggy and hung over, the soldiers stumbled out of the barn in various states of consciousness. Young George Shipley hid from the blushing Copus girls, his clothing and bedroll nowhere to be found. Only Launtze turned out in full kit, his musket half-cocked and shouldered. Copus pushed his way through the assembling men and handed Launtze a parched corn cob. "They were watching us last night," shouted the Reverend, laying his rifle against a stump. "I found the remains of a small fire about 400 yards to the East of us. They ate my corn and listened to the shindig. They could have had our scalps!"

"They didn't because there weren't no Indians!" objected Dye. "One small campfire is of no concern to us. There is not a damn Indian from here to Sandusky plains, Harrison saw to that, thank God," continued Dye as he unbuttoned his shirt. "If you need me, I'll be down at the spring."

Copus looked at Dye in astonishment. "I am warning you, George, you had better take your musket."

"Reverend, please, I can't kill Indians and bathe at the same time. It's physically impossible," Dye said sarcastically. The others laughed and stacked their arms against the barn door.

"Where I come from, the Devil holds no feast days," observed Launtze as he changed out his musket flint. "I shall stand guard with the Reverend."

Cold water ran from its rocky precipice, splashing over the backs of the rowdy bathers. Shipley quietly sat on a perch he had chosen atop a moss-covered log. He was wrapped in an undershirt borrowed from Copus's oldest son. An unsettling feeling came over him—something in the air, an odor. He could not place it, more animal than the familiar stink of his messmates' leather boots. When given the opportunity to wash he did not hesitate, taking his musket and kit with him. The others laughed at Shipley's appearance, cowing the boy into stacking his musket with the rest. He fearfully eyed the barn up the trail as the wind began to whistle around the hillside taking the odor with it. He could never live-down running to Copus for help.

Kanotchy held his breath to steady his aim. The musket, an old British Bess, trained on the naked back of George Dye. It offended him that Kratzer sent these small foolish boys to deal with the likes of him. There was no need for stealth, he realized, as the fiddler struck up a jig. Kanotchy's followers, forty in all, took up their positions among the rocks and thickets that choked the trail at its narrowest point between the cabin and the spring.

A jarring volley whistled through the bathing soldiers, knocking Dye into a clump of tall ferns at the end of the spring. Buck and ball sizzled overhead and riddled the torso of young Shipley who took a few labored steps before disappearing into the cloud of smoke. John Tedrick lay in a pool of blood, fitfully pleading for his life as two arms emerged from the noxious cloud and pulled him into the gray void.

Suddenly, a fury of musket fire resounded through the valley, unnerving Copus's dogs. Launtze grabbed his weapons and took up a position behind a stout apple barrel. Frantic, Copus pushed the last of the children into his small cabin where they would be safe—for now. "We best take cover inside," he shouted to Launtze who nodded his approval and stumbled backwards through the low doorway. Once inside, Copus tore open a greased paper window with the business end of his Kentucky rifle. A Delaware warrior stepped out from the tree line waving a bright red sash far above his head.

"Look at that," shouted Copus as he took aim through the partly open door!

"Don't shoot," snapped Launtze sighting down the barrel of his rifle. "They want to know the range of our weapons. You won't touch 'em at this distance."

"I have never seen such a thing," said the Reverend. "They mean to kill us!"

"Keep quiet! Unless you collect yourself, we are all done-for. Now put down that rifle and turn over the table. It will be our last defense."

Copus paused, closing his eyes momentarily. "Amy! Where is my wife?" Mrs. Copus pulled herself from their bewildered children and put a comforting hand on his shoulder. He smiled. "Place the young-uns up in the loft. Keep Wesley and Sarah behind the table. They will load; you pass the guns." Mrs. Copus gave her husband a worried nod and went to pluck an old large-bore musket from its place above the mantle. Sarah quietly pulled the shot box and horns from a pantry shelf and took the venerable weapon from her mother's hands. She quickly went to work ignoring harping pleas from her younger brother to join the coming fight.

From his position, hidden in ferns, Dye used his elbows to slither, snakelike, to an opening where he managed to glimpse the last advancing warrior vanishing into dense brush. Ignoring the burning wound that grazed his forehead he smeared away blood and grit from his eyelids to regain focus. To the left, atop the rocks, was what remained of Shipley, his bowels in a loose heap beneath his head. To his right lay the trampled path to the cabin.

Ahead, Tedrick's violin floated past its mangled owner and orbited near the tumbling water.

All four soldiers' muskets remained stacked against the rear of the barn, overlooked by the Natives as they took up new positions along the other side of the wall. Soon sharp reports of returned musket fire left two warriors dead among the forward pickets as they advanced and retreated to piercing rasps of staghorn rattles. Dye crawled into darkness under the barn's rear overhang and snatched-up Shipley's loaded weapon and kit. The war party inched its way forward, forming a pincer-like spread at the edge of the swaying corn. Dye took careful aim on a solitary Delaware who was guarding the raiders' nervous mounts. Then, under cover from heavy musketry, he fired unnoticed, knocking his target under the hoofs of rearing ponies.

Inside the Copus cabin the battle was fully engaged and becoming chaos. "You must load faster, damn it," shouted Copus forgetting himself in the deafening melee. Mrs. Copus was choking on thick smoke behind him, scraping the pan of an empty musket. "Sarah," she shouted to the terrified and flustered girl, "lay on the floor and slide me your kit." Wesley smacked Sarah on the head and took her powder horn to his mother behind the toppled bench.

"Look," cried Launtze peering through an opening he had made in the chinking! Copus broke his aim steadying the rifle on his hip while unbolting the door.

Dye howled like a banshee diving through the open door like one of the missiles flying everywhere around him. The warrior blocking his path fell dead. Copus caught the wounded soldier in his arms then gasped and staggered backwards against the door. Dye, realizing the gravity of the situation shouted for Wesley to get his father's gun and take over as he pulled the wounded preacher to the rope bed at the rear of the cabin.

"What have I done?" repeated Copus, tightening his grip on Dye's forearm. "I cannot move my legs." Mrs. Copus choked back tears as she propped up his head with the family Bible.

"Do not strain yourself," she whispered softly. "The lord will guide you into the light."

"I see nothing, Amy," muttered the Reverend as he closed his eyes. Sarah screamed then sobbed uncontrollable as her mother recited prayers in her native German.

"For God's sake take the women up to the loft," ordered Launtze ending the vigil. Looking to align another shot, he could find none. The battle had stopped as suddenly as it had begun. Inside the cabin there was only wound-binding, cries of pain, stunned exhaustion and grief.

Kanotchy paced the edge of the tree line, extending then collapsing his battered spyglass in a nervous rhythm. The youngest warriors labored past, dragging their dead and dying to the remaining ponies. "Their holy man is dying," said Tom Lyons, a gnarled and war-scarred elder, as he emerged from tall grass at the corner of the field. This mauve painted apparition brushed past Kanotchy and relieved himself behind a nearby tree. "Let us finish this thing before the sun is overhead."

"The end has been decided," replied Kanotchy as he took the reins of his mount and signaled the men to fall back. Lyons shook his head. "We must burn the cabin first."

"We have bled the Holy Man white," interrupted Kanotchy looking through his glass at the battered dwelling. "It is finished. We will gather at Goshen." All fell silent. "Ride to the English camp at Malden and tell the Captain of our victory. He will give us guns and men. Make haste."

A veil of smoke drifted slowly upward, exposing shattered wood and bloodstains outside the Copus cabin as Captain Martin arrived with his detail of men. They had heard the battle and assumed it was Dye and his fellows target practicing. "Damn fool of a parson," scowled Martin from his prancing mount, viewing Copus's body as a burial detail carried it out. "A pity he could not stay put."

"The devils are headed southeast," groaned Launtze nursing his shattered arm in the doorway. "Looked to be fifty of em." Martin waived him off. "What of the rest of our party?"

"George Dye is up in the loft with a wounded knee. The ball passed through, striking one of the Copus girls in the thigh. The others never returned from the spring."

"There is an old animal trail that runs along the Black Fork then turns south," said Jacob Beam as he pulled a jug from his saddle bag. "Follow me and we will be upon them in an hour."

"You are a miller, not an officer," said Martin gravely. "They outnumber us. No, we will make camp and bury our dead."

A Forest of Eyes—Laylan's Journey

William Gass was an intimidating man with arms like tree trunks and a wide barrel chest. His face was flush and worn from the effects of ceaseless toil. He boasted that in a little less than a week he and his sons and brothers, had built the imposing blockhouse that now safeguarded his small family cabin and spring. Laylan sat uncomfortably at the crowded table, half listening to the ramblings of his animated host while Mrs. Gass plucked the last skillet from its seat in the dying embers.

Gass was speaking, "Captain Martin is a humbug!" His pronouncement created a pause during which he spooned another helping of pot pie. "Where I come from courtesy is the rule you understand. My mother, God rest her soul, instilled in me a belief that having nothing good to say, you keep your mouth shut. I have faithfully lived by this rule—mind you Martin is the exception—a humbug!"

Mrs. Gass turned away from her intoxicated husband and served Laylan another slice of cornbread. Smiling eagerly, he crumbled the dense bread into gravy and mashed it all together with a spoon. "I cannot thank you enough for your hospitality," he said, shoveling down the last vestige of hs meal. "I can't remember the last time I ate so well. I've had but a handful of berries these last two days." The children stared at the odd appearance of their ragged guest.

"I've never seen a sunburn like that," chuckled young Benjamin. "Is there any part of you that isn't beet red?"

"Perhaps," shrugged Laylan, "but that's for me to know." Mrs. Gass turned flush at the insinuation and banished her young from the raucous gathering. Across the table Winn Winship discretely eased his plate under the bench allowing the Gass's hounds a feast of fat and gristle.

"John Chapman stopped me outside of Fredericktown last week in quite a lather," said the postmaster, meeting the glare of Mrs. Gass. You would have thought the world was about to end. The death of Mr. Jones was lamentable to be sure, but to spread rumors of invasion? Well sir, it's balderdash, nothing more. The man should be wholly ignored." Mr. Gass stood up as if to speak only to be interrupted a second time by Winship. "To excite the populace with such tales... I had a chance to meet with Mr. Pardy of Huron who assured me that the English-Canadian 'invasion' was nothing more than a prisoner exchange." Gass nudged Laylan sharply passing him the jug.

"I have been told that Mr. Winship soiled himself that night," whispered Gass, "and shot Isach Arres's milk cow with his lady's pistol thinking it was a redcoat—the fop."

"I must thank you for your hospitality, Mrs. Gass said Winship removing his wig, "and now I shall like to retire. Could you show me to my cot?" Mr. Gass shook his head. "You will sleep on the floor near the hearth like all of our guests." Winship grudgingly removed his long coat carefully spreading it on the ground. "My God man! Do you not have bedding of any kind?"

"Bedding?" mumbled Gass, taking another drink. "About a month ago we buried a squatter, a rough by the name of Dyle—bear hunter I think. Well, Mr. Dyle made his home in an old wigwam he found out on the Clearfork not far from here. One night a band of cutthroats found him sleeping-off the cider, still as death. Well sir, this Mr. Dyle was a real son-of-a-bitch you understand, not the kind of man you rob and let live—a killer in his own right."

"Is this subject necessary?" interrupted Winship rubbing his eyes.

"It most certainly is!" replied Gass. "Especially if you travel unarmed through these parts like Mr. Laylan! Now where was I? Ah, so the cutthroats made themselves at home, you see, stripping his camp of everything practical, and when the last jug had been emptied they trussed old Dyle up in his bedding and set it ablaze. He must have been good and pickled as I saw no signs of a struggle nor did I hear his screams the night before. We are no strangers to death, Mr. Laylan, but to share Dyle's fate would be a horrible thing. Had he been sober the devils would have had to shoot him—a better end, I think."

Winship sat up. "Why have I not heard of this Mr. Dyle?"

"Do you question these events, Mr. Winship?

"No, not in the least," said Winship, "What I question is your timing. Are we in peril?"

Gass smiled as he extinguished the last candle with his fingertips. "Don't think on it. We used to see their camp fires at night, just across the creek at the edge of our property—a little too close for my taste. Now they cower in a deep ravine well out of our sight. We leave a lantern burning in the upper gallery of our little fort every night. It keeps them thinking we are garrisoned."

"That is hardly a comfort," prodded Winship resting his head on a canvas mailbag. "Had I known of this I would have demanded an escort. Thieves and cutthroats—what stuff!"

Gass pulled off his knee boots and rested them at an angle against the fire dog. "You need not fret, Winship, your marksmanship is legend even in these parts. Ha! Well, I have no more energy for ribbing. Glare at Mr. Laylan if you wish. As for me, the comforts of bed and wife await. Good night gentlemen."

"I should have pushed on to Mansfield," groused Winship who finally closed his eyes. "What stuff indeed!"

At dawn, near the spring, a brooding owl watched the labored movements of a straggling mole from atop its chestnut perch, then suddenly took flight as Mrs. Gass approached a towering wood pile with an ax over her shoulder. From the lowlands an impregnable mist spread its ashen hand and obscured the small homestead from the coming light.

Laylan pulled himself from the hard-packed floor casting-off the snoring postman's wandering leg. "I will never drink another drop," he thought as he rubbed his beating temples. This did nothing to retard the ever-sharpening headache radiating from behind his eyes, or dull the percussive strikes of splitting cordwood ringing through the small open windows. Mrs. Gass could wield an ax as well as any man, observed Laylan from the narrow doorway. Her long sinewy figure and sun-cured complexion reminded him of an Indian maiden, or a mulatto.

"How long have you been watching me?" shouted Mrs. Gass leaning the ax against a large stump. "I'm sorry, there is no hot chicory as of yet. A man is useless without his morning cup. Believe me, I know."

"Don't trouble yourself on my account", said Laylan. "I just wanted to thank you and your husband for the hospitality you have shown me. Is Bill not yet awake?"

"Oh yes," replied Mrs. Gass wiping down her forehead with the hem of her patchwork apron. "He left before sun-up with his favorite dog—went squirrel hunting I think. Would you like a plate of cold mush? It's inside the pantry—or maybe some apples?"

"An apple or two should hold me till afternoon. Anyway, I'm sorry I have no coin to offer for your kindness."

"Look around," said Mrs. Gass hoisting the ax once again. "What would I do with coin? In these parts lead has more value than gold or silver—a pity. What I would not give for a silken gown or a Sunday shawl. Forgive me if I dream, Mr. Laylan. This is a Godless country. What good are these things without society? If my mother in heaven were to gaze upon me now, she would not recognize me. It takes faith, Mr. Laylan, to think anything is to come of this toil and misery. Oh, there is one request I should like to make if it is not too much to ask—more of a favor. In the upper loft of the blockhouse you will find in the rafters a nice bruin ham hanging up with the onions and dried goods. It goes to the miller, a Mr. Watson who lives downstream of the nearest ford. Just follow the Clearfork. It is, after all, a stop along your way. My husband would do it but he doesn't get along with the miller too well. Bill blames his tooth ailments on the amount of grit in his meal. Bill is a man of poor habits and irksome hygiene. I try to tell him that the pipe and jug are the source of his ills, but that does neither of us much good—you can't force anything from an old mule, that is certain."

"The fog is lifting," said Laylan abruptly, "and I must be on my way. I will give the miller your husband's highest regards."

Mrs. Gass grinned, reaching for the water ladle. "That will bring hoots of laughter to the Watson's table to be sure."

From the spring an ancient footpath twisted through sumac, vanishing at times into patches of flowering goldenrod. Legions of orb spiders labored like mariners aloft, netting one green stalk to another as they rigged and mended damp webs for today's catch. Laylan pushed deeper into the lowland vegetation easing the pungent ham from one spot to another on his aching shoulder. Through the milky haze loomed a distant tree line, revealing the course of the Clear Fork as it wound its way across the mottled valley. Sounds of nature were soon joined by groaning from the mill's great wheel as it powered the sawmill and its busy blade, which rose and fell in monotonous rhythm. At this crude sawpit, trees which had swayed and creaked through centuries of storms were now being unceremoniously fashioned into cogs and gears—the instruments of their ultimate destruction.

The trail, increasingly steep, had taken Laylan to a broad rise above the flood plain where he rested for a moment on a smoothed contour of river rock, one of a dozen or so lonely monuments placed over the bones of Native hunters, long forgotten.

"You had better state your business," hailed a voice from beyond the trees. "Speak up, damn you, or I'll put a ball between your eyes, now raise your hands where I can see them." Laylan obeyed, slowly coming to his feet.

"For God's sake lower your rifle," said Laylan to the man in the shadows. "I am a friend of Mr. Gass. Do you know him?"

"That remains to be seen," replied the voice. "Where is your weapon?"

"I bear only this bruin ham," shrugged Laylan, "In payment to a Mr. Watson from the Gass household."

"A ham is not a practical weapon," growled the millwright, stepping into the sun, "unless consumed of course." Watson scratched his neck and lowered his rifle. "Well sir, it's not pork, but who can afford to eat that right now, not with the government paying four dollars a barrel." The millwright winced as he sniffed the ham. "At least the redskins will barter for it. They seem to have a taste for all things off-putting, God knows. I've made a small fortune trading with them in the past, but I guess those days have ended." Watson frowned, biting off a chaw. "The squatters that remain would just as soon stab you in the back as make a transaction. At least their womenfolk have a sense for business. If it were not so, I would be stuck with this putrid ham. Well friend, I have squawked on long enough. There is much work to be done. You should come along and fill your canteens at out still house. I can't allow a blowhard like Gass to be more inviting than me."

Watson's saw pit sat low in the dimly lit valley, half hidden between two large stands of girdled chestnuts destined for the woodsman's ax. A  small low-hanging shed built of rough poles and clapboard housed the crude machinery which noisily drove a single reciprocating blade. Watson brushed past Laylan and wrenched open the sluiceway's wooden gate. Water gushed through the narrow locks, sending the breast-wheel into a faster rotation. Watson bore little resemblance to the image of a swarthy backwoods miller, Laylan thought, as they slowly made their way into the shade of the little millhouse. He was of no great height—no larger than young Ben Gass. His skin was yellow and waxen, chafed red in patches by abrasion from his coarse tow cloth blouse. Mr. Watson carried the mark of ill health seldom seen in a man in his 20's. Still, there was an air of violent confidence from this hardened pioneer, his knife and rifle always within easy reach. Watson's younger brother, Noah, struggled with the spike of an iron peavy, rocking it a little at a time beneath a great beech log, cursing and levering and cajoling its leading edge into the relentless teeth of the hungry metal saw. Noticing a manpower shortage, Laylan stripped to the waist and joined Watson and his wife at the rear of the log. Watson footed one end of a wooden spar, twice the length of the wooden channel under the log. On the count of three they raised the spar above their heads and drove the log at a slow uneven pace through the smoking blade, a process repeated until there was nothing left but rough planks.

The miller offered advice as he inspected his yield. "It would be wise to start for McCleur's blockhouse as soon as you are able. It's a hard five miles or so downstream of us. When Captain Walker marched his men through these parts not two months ago he placed my brother Samuel in charge of the blockhouse guard. Samuel is a fussy one—does everything by the manual. So, unless you plan on sleeping with the wolves, I would get to the outpost before he bolts the door at dusk."

"McCleur…The last time I came south I boarded at his cabin. It took a solid week for my head to stop spinning," recalled Laylan with a touch of guilt. "Say what you will about the quality of his boarders, it's the flow of whiskey that interests me most."

"That may be," sighed Watson "but it was an illegal venture altogether, something my brother put a halt-to the moment he stepped into that shack town with a commission. It is lamentable if you ask me. McCleur is an honest upright man after all. And as for my brother Samuel, well he has designs of his own. The still house over yonder, that's of Samuel's own construction."

Noah glared at Watson. "McCleur should have known better, being a man of law and all." Watson waved him off, turning his attention back to Laylan.

"There will be more than enough business for everyone once we settle things with the British. Then we can all grow fat together."

"Oh for the love of God," erupted Noah angrily; "everybody knows you can't grow an extra chin with a gut full of tapeworms! Redskins, McCleurs, makes no damn difference in my eyes. I tell you we must draw them out or waste away to nothing."

Watson yawned, handing Laylan back his shirt and hat from the high shelf above the tool chest. "I for one believe, Mr. Laylan, that when the dust has cleared, hotheads like Noah here will soon come to miss the redskin method of trade. They will be replaced by even shrewder cheats and louts soon enough. And as for McCleur, well he's no different than myself, and that's the truth of it. When we settled into this wilderness no heed was paid to any laws. I still don't know, or care for that matter, what they are, and neither does Noah or Samuel. You can be assured, sir, that when the weather turns foul and my patrons seek shelter, I give them a drink of whiskey and a place by the hearth to lay down, no different than McCleur, Gass or anyone else who values future patronage. It's as simple as that."

"It must be difficult to be at such odds with your own kin," said Laylan as he knocked the dust from the brim of his hat.

Watson turned his attention to the darkening shadow of restless passenger pigeons moving en-masse high above the tiny mill. "Difficulty?" repeated Watson lost in thought. "They each have a separate notion of how to make their fortunes out here—leaving me always for want of help. Why, my wife's hands have grown so calloused from pushing timber that I reel from her touch at night."

"Thank God she's out of earshot," snickered Noah. "I think Amariah's worried she'll grow a beard before too long."

Noah smiled at Laylan, motioning him down a trampled path to a small clearing below the mill dam's log embankment. "Forgive my brother for prattling on like an old Whig," said Noah as he pushed away a pile of branches revealing a small strip-built canoe hidden away in the miller's refuse. "I toil every day at my brother's side without the benefit of wage or property. At least Samuel has his freedom—I've said too much."

Laylan slowly circled the craft, stopping at intervals to shake the frame lashings and gunwales. "You would do well to store her hull-up before the bottom rots all the way through," he observed while lifting the bow.

"It belongs to Samuel," explained Noah. "He said he got it upstream of us from a Wyandot lad—traded a couple of stew pots and a shovel for it—or so he says."

"Very interesting," nodded Laylan, folding his arms, "but why show me?"

"Just let me continue," hastened Noah. "Last week Samuel sent a volunteer from the blockhouse to collect it, but Amariah had holed her on a snag the night before. Well, Amariah filled the soldier full of whiskey and double-talk and sent him back to shack town empty-handed while I labored away with hot pitch and tow cloth just to get her floating again."

"Have you succeeded?" interrupted Laylan who was impatient to continue on his journey.

"She leaks like a sieve," laughed Noah, "but my brother still needs her. Boating down the forks remains the fastest way to get from his post to Mount Vernon—at least when the water's high. You can take her down to McCleur's and deliver her to Samuel. It'll save you some time."

"You are placing a lot of trust in a stranger," said Laylan, pulling the fragile craft into a shallow pool away from the gnarled bank.

"Trust," laughed Noah out loud, "I don't need to trust you, no sir. It's more of an act of courtesy. You get to rest your legs from here to McCleur's place, where the guard has set up stations along the banks. If it floats, they'll seize it. Trust, you see, is no longer a burden to us. Just keep an open eye for log jams and such."

Tangled willow boughs swayed from straining branches and formed latticed arches of dappled colors. A cool breeze whispered ghostly verses through the dark valley, dropping beech nuts and faded leaves upon the parting men. Along the banks a community of squirrels increased their meager stashes, taking little notice of Laylan or the quarreling millers on the far shore.

Laylan drove a push-pole down into the murky stream bed maneuvering unsteadily into deeper water. There was little need to paddle, he quickly observed, as the current gripped the narrow craft and accelerated him through the swollen tributary, leaving the mill and its irksome politics behind the boat's gurgling wake. He leaned back uncomfortably into its leaking hull, narrowly avoiding the swooping talons of branches flailing like ugly daggers from above.

A cold bead of water slowly bled through the canoe's thin hull, soon saturating the mat of rushes on which he knelt. Laylan stayed at eye level with the gunwale and turned the paddle blade hard against the current in an unexpected scramble to steer the ungainly craft. For a moment he lost his balance, swinging the canoe stern-first through a gauntlet of stumps and boulders. Frantic, the seasoned sailor struggled for control as the canoe began to sideslip through a pack of churning debris, tearing the paddle from his battered hands. Foam and silted water poured over the foundering craft sweeping away the rough sack holding his boots and scant provisions. Instinctively Laylan scrambled for the high side of the canoe, sinking it in an instant beneath the roiling water, taking him down with it. He began to panic. To drown, he had always imagined, involved a certain acceptance, a few moments to exhale the last of your breath before succumbing to the inevitable. But this was a gnawing violent death. Laylan's thoughts grew incoherent, becoming suffused with an animal's struggle to claw its way to the churning surface.

Through closed eyes a cabin materialized out of the darkness, its form growing more familiar with every step to the door. Laylan had expelled the last contents of his lungs and had given-in to the Clearfork's malevolent hold. Slowly turning in an ethereal haze, all was darkness except for a dim yellow light streaming from the threshold, where, to his delight, the gaunt silhouette of his daughter played in the flickering shadows. Laylan smiled as he entered and placed his hat on its usual perch at the corner of the mantle.

A sudden jolt of crushing pain ripped him from his phantasm as the cabin and all its warmth transformed into cold rushing water. He gasped for air writhing snakelike onto a ledge of jumbled roots extending, half submerged, from the opposing bank. His left shoulder grew numb and throbbed with each breath. As he drew himself onto the bank, blood oozed from a wound and attracted a swarm of gnats. He once more closed his eyes. This time there were no visions, only an overwhelming urge to rest.

One sharp prod soon followed by another stronger jab jolted Laylan from his respite among the fallen leaves. A lonely-looking ill-fed girl in Native garb came into focus standing before him. She glanced pensively over her shoulder toward the tree line at her back.

Laylan winced as he asked, "Can you help me to my feet?" The girl looked him over, particularly his battered shoulder. "Can you guide me to a road?" he whispered anxiously. To this she made no reply other than to push him backward with all her strength onto a bed of yellow leaves. He inquired again only to get the same response along with her continuing and frustrating silence. She studied him intently from her perch on a nearby rock where she unsheathed a small rusted knife from the crest of her leggings. Laylan did not stir, allowing the mysterious girl a moment to calm her fears before either of them acted rashly.

"Can you even understand me?" he called out to his new companion. The girl nodded in reply and cut a narrow thong of fabric from the hem of her tunic. This she drew tightly around Laylan's bleeding shoulder, sealing the leaking bandage with mud from the slippery bank.

Dry brush cracked under an unseen foot startling a great blue heron from its stance in the stream and signaling the arrival of more company.

The sounds grew louder and prompted Laylan's rescuer to run to an open clearing where she waved her arms letting loose a crazed guttural scream eliciting an ambuscade of well-armed men. Emerging from their hiding places in the dense underbrush, they quickly flanked Laylan and the girl. "Are you the blockhouse guard?" asked Laylan nervously. A sharp jab in the ribs with a blunderbuss silently answered his question as he was pulled to his feet. They were not the blockhouse guard, but a small rag-tag group of toughs dressed in an odd mixture of Indian, trapper and military garb. Two men pulled him to his feet. Cold steel, now pressing impatiently against his tail-bone pushed him forward into the dark constricting wilderness. A strong metallic scent wafted through the trees enveloping the group and their captive with the pungent stench of blood and fire.

The party halted, then changed direction into the path of the noxious smoke. The carcass of a large split and stinking sow bruin hung from a branch, its rank fat sputtering actively as it dribbled down into the faint orange glow of a brush and dung fire. Without warning, Laylan's captor swung his weapon around like a club bashing him across his swelling wound. Laylan fell to the ground in agony where the barrel of the gun came down on him a second time, smashing into his shoulder blade with a thud. "Allow me the pleasure of introduction," said one of the men with a heavy French accent. "You may refer to me as Monsieur Light. I apologize for your treatment at our hands, but these are dark times you see, and these days it is quite impossible to tell friend from foe. As for you, monsieur, I do not yet know where you stand." Laylan slowly raised his head from the mud fearing another violent strike from behind. Monsieur Light curtly stepped over Laylan and crouched down to eye level with his wounded prey. "And you red hair, have provided me no introduction, eh? Is there anything I should know about you?"

"I have nothing to offer," Laylan said angrily, "and I am no threat to you for Christ's sake. I have no musket, not even a pair of boots on my feet.

"That, I can readily see," said Light testily, "perhaps you have deserted this armed mob Harrison calls a legion-eh? Perhaps you are a spy— but no! Surely this could not be." Light smiled and helped Laylan to his feet. "You are lucky we found you when we did. Your shoulder seems to be in quite a state and it is not such a good day for swimming—no?" Light broke eye contact motioning the girl to his side. "This is my daughter Magdeline. She is sadly a mute—the very image of her parted mother, an Indian maiden of great beauty."

"Yes, yes a rose among thistles I'm sure," interrupted Laylan through his pain, "and what of my captors? Are they mutes as well?"

"No, no!" shrugged Light exchanging glances with his men. "They are not men of words, so to speak, so I speak for them—believe me it is for the best. That being said, I must ask you a second time, what brings you to my river?" Light leaned into Laylan and peered deeply into his eyes. Laylan gave no answer, but glared as if to say "none of your business."

"No matter," said the Frenchman dusting himself off. "Sooner or later we must all make our way to the river. Whether we sink into its murk or reach the other side—well, that's never really in our hands. Is this not so, red hair? I am asking you, is this not so?"

"I have had enough of your salon talk!" growled Laylan through clenched teeth. "Now are you going to kill me or let me on my way?"

"I do not wish to kill you, monsieur," replied Light watching the girl adjust Laylan's bandage. "I never kill men for so little. That is what separates my kind from you backwoods English. I would rather barter, monsieur, than to take what I have to take. The local settlements get nervous—and that is not so good for me. I barter with them for my living. What a shame it was that dear Magdaline could not just leave you to your business."

"Well put," agreed Laylan.

Light turned his back to Laylan, wiping his hands on a dirty swatch of calico rag. "Still, my wounded friend, there must be made a transaction, for the good of all. Tell me, Red, that ring upon your finger, it is silver, no?"

"I think you know what silver looks like," said Laylan twisting the band from his finger.

"A wedding band," announced Light in mock delight as he held it up for all to see. The others took little interest in such a paltry offering and one-by-one filed back into the obscurity of the noxious smoke. "Not many men care to show their appreciation. Not out here anyway... No, in this land of milk and manna such tokens are nothing more than scrap, a mere pittance. No, monsieur. It is not enough."

"I have had my fill of this!" said Laylan. "Give me a blanket for the damned ring and be done with it."

"I have need of every rag in my possession, you understand," replied Light, his fingers now tapping an impatient rhythm on the large pistol stuffed haphazardly into his sash. "That knife," enquired the Frenchman expectedly, "the one you wear in your belt. I would like that as well. Maybe there is something I could give you. Would you like to see the girl alone? I would not impose..."

Magdeline reluctantly left Light's side for Laylan's steady arm, slowly guiding his hand to the small wooden buttons of her dirty tunic. Laylan recoiled from the girl's clumsy advances letting loose a sudden cry of pain as his shoulder extended.

"Your daughter's honor for a carving knife," said Laylan in disgust. "I need shoes, Light, not a roll in the hay. For Christ sake, I'll settle for a canteen of water."

"No!" replied Light as he scrutinized the tarnished ring. "No, I relish the shoes upon my feet, nor can I spare good water. And as for the girl, you needn't worry about her honor, monsieur, that veil was lifted on the first night of your invasion of Canada. I believe it was the only possession you backwoods bandits managed to liberate. I personally do not understand your kind, or your famous sense of honor. You rape, plunder then retreat. That is all you English Yankee types are good for. You are all the same, and that is why my friend, the Devil Napoleon, cannot be halted. In Europe he eats the British vandals for his supper, you see, while you Yankees cannot defeat their Redcoats on your soil, even though they are the worst English soldiers, and they are so few. Perhaps I should just kill you and feed you to the wolves. That could put my mind at ease. What do you think?"

"I think I have had enough!" roared Laylan seizing Magdeline by the throat. "You will, by God step aside!" Magdeline gagged and choked violently through his tightening grip as she desperately fought for air. "God has damned me!" ranted Laylan to the surprised Frenchman, "Damned me as if I've been undermined—by hams, canoes, and now," he stammered drawing his knife, "and now by orations from a cutthroat pimp. I can bear it no longer."

"You think you are Job, eh?" replied Light. "Tell me Job, what will you do now?" Light moved closer, his eyes black and unflinching. "Monsieur," he spoke softly into Laylan's ear. "Perhaps I have frightened you beyond reason. Perhaps I should not have pushed you so. You now have, after all, the upper hand." Light chuckled and slapped Laylan hard on the back. "I guess you have smoked me." Laylan roared out in pain dropping the long knife harmlessly into the mud between Magdeline's kicking feet. "Pardon monsieur, we seem to be at— oh how do you say it—ah an impasse. You have dropped your only possession and yet you will not let go of mine. Behind you is only the river. You must believe me when I tell you it cares not for our poor possessions. Why don't you release the girl and take your chances on the miller's trail? It's surely safer than the currents when the water is wild like today. If you wish I will even point the way."

Laylan nervously broke eye contact as Light's compatriots busied themselves in the shade, hacking to pieces the smoldering bruin carcass with tomahawks and broad axes, its blackened portions tossed with little care into the depths of a dirty tow cloth sack.

"You have wasted my time," said Light as he took up a singed knob of flesh from the bag, "yet I must pity you now." He sniffed and inspected the fatty morsel carefully before chewing it down. "Personally, I cannot understand how your kind can stomach such fare. Me, monsieur, I prefer haddock and champagne—forgive me, I should not jest."

Laylan leaned in toward Magdeline's ear to reassure her. "I am sorry for this. I do not want to hurt you."

"It is time to let go," said Light wearily. "I see that we have no further dealings, you and I." At his nod an imposing Delaware spat out his portion of the kill and wrestled Magdeline from Laylan's grasp. "I have decided to grant you quarter," said Light picking up the knife. "This was, after all, an unfortunate misunderstanding in the most unfortunate of times. No doubt you have pressing business downstream, and as your host I will delay you no further. To stress his sincerity Light handed the knife over to Laylan and turned his back. "Now you must return to the south bank of the river. There along the crest you will find a scarcely trodden path which is much preferable to the snags below, and as for this meeting of ours...."

"I have had nothing in my travels but hardship and wild beasts," admitted Laylan as he started for the trail.

"Well put!" shouted the Frenchman now out of sight. He took one last look at the ring and carefully put it in a velvet pouch around his neck.

"Are we just to let him go then?" prodded the warrior as he took up his tomahawk from the mound of steaming offal. "His scalp is worth one, maybe two muskets at Malden—this I know to be the truth."

"Malden you say," erupted Light. "Damn that feral cancer. Malden, my friend, is a long way from this place—no! I will hear no more of Malden... Perhaps Captain Watson is expecting our man tonight. Have you thought of that, Eh? Is he a blockhouse runner? Perhaps he is a relative of our dear Captain. Well my friend, that is what we do not know and that is why I am content to just let him on his way." Light paused a moment clapping his hand onto the Wyandot's sturdy shoulder. "We are nothing to him, you see, just mistaken, ignorant hunters. That is all. If we kill him then we cease to be invisible."

"Invisible?" repeated the Wyandot through clenched teeth. "I do not think you or the girl understand its meaning. I have listened to your fancy pronouncements and find they are nothing more than words—yes words fit for a drunken chief or politician. Was it your girl who found the red-haired man? Yes it was. A mute girl should count stealth as an advantage. I ask you, Light, why she made herself known to him. I could have silenced him then but you wished to give the stranger life and free him. I say you are no chieftain, Light, and I say you have not the strength to pass such judgements."

"You complain of my leadership—yes?" fumed Light now stuffing loose tobacco into the cracked bowl of a long calumet. "I very much prefer your usual silence in such matters. Savages, I have found, are at their noblest when sober and obedient. Remember this, my friend, that you travel with me because your way of life and your Native principles have withered away with the changing leaves. It is your physical strength, not brashness that will sustain your life when there is finally nothing left to hunt." Light fired the moist tobacco handing off the long pipe, stem first, through a thickening cloud of smoke.

"The red-haired man has not gone far," interrupted the unconvinced Wyandot shoving aside the noxious offering. "I can still hear the branches snapping beneath his feet. Let me kill him, Light, or the stranger will be the death of us all."

"I have heard enough," bristled Light, his command once more challenged. "I do not wish to make a damned game of this matter. Kill him quickly, and Two Dogs, use cold steel! Take your scalp and for God's sake bury him deep in the mud. No one must hear or suspect a thing!"

"Dead cats don't mew," the warrior replied shouldering his blunderbuss. "You surprise me, Light. I did not think you knew my name." Light quietly dipped his fingertips against the blackened edge of the fire pit, anointing with reverence Two Dogs' face and chest, forming a war pattern in warm grey ash.

"If I did not know your name," replied Light looking him up and down, "I could never trust so much in you. Now, take along the others and make your hunt quick. I will break camp and drink to your swift return."

"God damn me!" Laylan cursed to himself a second time. It was only with pious caution that he withdrew the next blasphemy now forming against the tip of his tongue. The river, that serpentine path preferred by so many, had gradually become snarled with bristled foliage choking and obscuring the current's edge, it tendrils forming a high abattis of impregnable briar.

A cool breeze, welcome at first, coursed erratically through the dimly lit valley, rattling bush tops against the drooping willow boughs that shaded the windward bank. The effect was disorienting as it silenced even the Clearfork's familiar roar. Laylan dropped to his knees, sinking painfully into the soft punk of a rotted stump, causing a tumult of panic among the carpenter ants residing deep beneath the upholstery of moss. A moment of clarity came only in absolute stillness, his ears now adjusting to the woodland clamor he had found so disorienting while on the move. There was, albeit faint, a distant yet familiar clap of ringing axes. All soon went quiet as the wind abated for a moment. Laylan heard the familiar scraping, creaking cacophony of leaves and branches crushing understory brush, followed by the crashing of a great oak or chestnut hurtling to the forest floor. "Lousetown," smiled Laylan as he scrambled to his feet. Water can conduct distant sounds, a fact which as a sailor he knew only too well. He last noticed this aboard the *Sally*, six months earlier, as he lay aloft, sent into action by the nasal piping of beat-to-quarters, an order given by a British sloop of war six or eight miles downwind of them. Just as before, there was little time to waste.

The stranger's erratic trail now pleased Two Dogs in a way that both irked and confused his tiring fellow hunters who were straggling further behind. It was not for their well-being or his own nagging aches that he had come to a sudden stop. The scent—its bittersweet aroma—had once-more returned with the shifting breeze. Two Dogs suppressed a smile, and with a roll of his hand wafted the odor to his nose as it rose from a shapeless set of tracks. This was no chance find, nor was it in any way a mystical gift from his ancestors, as the others had come to believe. The stranger, to Two Dogs' delight, had stepped on the bear's swollen gall while leaving camp, smashing it to a pulp, releasing its scent. It was Light's most valuable share of the kill. And now, he smirked, the Frenchman's profits would guide him to a much more honorable trophy. It did not require the nose of a dog or guidance of a long-dead patriarch, just an awareness of the significance of this ever-so-faint perfume. The others, totally bamboozled, stood back now, reverently awaiting his somber divination as Two Dogs tasted the muddled ground before staring-down his rapt audience. "The red-haired man is losing the last of his strength," he declared, borrowing the Frenchman's pomp. "The spirits of the air, and those of the earth have so told me."

"Our Lord in heavin," sputtered a hushed voice in whisper. Gem James stared at Two Dogs in stunned amazement as he slowly made the sign of the cross on his bare chest. The burley Irishman, a deserter, uttered a short prayer to himself, his left hand never leaving the pommel of an old butcher's knife. "What will the spirits have us do now?" asked James without hesitation.

"They wish us to take the red-haired man as a tribute," muttered Two Dogs as if still entranced. "Alarm no one. Let the settler's children find his head amongst the fallen chestnuts in the morning." Two Dogs paused a moment looking into the eyes of all assembled. "Our medicine lies within the stranger's living breath; so we will lift it, not for ourselves, but as an offering to our forefathers, guiding us here."

"This I do for my sons not yet born," added the trembling voice of another. Two Dogs came quickly to his feet, brandishing a tomahawk high above the heads of his kneeling men. "And now we will become wolves," he growled, repeating the words in a chant until his speech transformed into the howl of a ravenous canine. The wild-eyed men took the cue, vanishing wisplike into the tangled underbrush. Two Dogs contorted his body into the form of a snarling beast, shedding all that was not necessary for the final kill, and with the flat of his knife in his teeth, stalked on calloused elbows towards the settlement's only landing.

Across the river on a low bluff stood the remains of Judge McCleur's still-house, a once familiar destination now a skeleton of bare poles and lumber. Two Dogs sensed something was amiss as his eyes strained for a better view. At first glance, nothing seemed out of the ordinary. Men went about their tasks with an air of enjoyment brought on no doubt by the seductive aroma of a roasting steer. Was this some kind of occasion? His stomach began to growl involuntarily as a rich scent wafted at intervals across the water. This was no ordinary work party. Arms were stacked in neat gleaming rows against the blockhouse hitching post. These were not the long rifles carried by local militia, but spit-polished federal arms, bayonets fixed.

Another sycamore cracked loudly then fell to a crash on the muddy flood plain which sloped upwards from settlement's flowing boundaries. Men soon poured over the fallen giant like hungry beasts, dismembering branches from the trunk, heaping them alive onto a fire, producing acrid smoke which hung close to the ground and swirled submissively around the boots of triumphant ax men.

All this clearing had created a gap on the hillside into which an officer and his staff soon appeared. From the shadows Two Dogs watched uneasily as the well-dressed Lieutenant lifted a gleaming brass instrument out of an open box, affixing it carefully to the mountings of a stout tripod. The officer stared motionless for long intervals at the strange instrument, conferring with another soldier who took notes on an unfurled map.

Gem James cursed, sheathing his tomahawk in frustration. Downstream a bit, two naked engineers waded gingerly into the swollen riffles, forcing themselves through the bracing current to a section of crude pilings dotting the Clearfork midstream. The officer ashore took another long reading from the polished instrument, hailing the now suffering engineers as they labored to replant a heavy iron guide rod back into the officer's line of sight.

"There is nothing for us here," James whispered to Two Dogs as he turned his back on the settlement, quitting the ambush.

"My knife has been tempered in the blood of worthier men," replied Two Dogs hotly. "I say we need not fear such scribblers or the soldiers that back them."

"That is because you are ignorant of their sciences," whispered James, his eyes fixed once more on the officer taking sightings. The Irishman chose his words with great care. "I had been in the service of the King since a lad of fourteen. I know what they are doing. They will advance, gazing into their instruments all the while, laying open this land both on the ground and on that paper as a busy route for their many purposes. We must quit this place as God himself can nay change their designs."

"Quiet!" snapped the Wyandot, clinging to his plan, throwing James back into the thicket of ripening sumac and pinning his back with a knee. But the time for cold steel had passed. Two Dogs dropped his tomahawk next to James as snapping twigs grabbed his attention. His right thumb and forefinger instinctively slid to the scatter gun's frizzen, located the flint, and with a sharp snap pulled the steel dog to a full cock.

James struggled under the Wyandot's boot in a futile attempt to leave. "Do not so much as twitch," whispered the nervous warrior, his ears pinpointing movements in the wilderness behind him. There were scramblings of creatures displaced by the smoke and noise of the soldier's reverie, but there was something else.

Suddenly the snapping was upon them, an explosion, like the charge of a bull, knocked the two men aside in a desperate push to the moving river beyond. Recovering, Two Dogs stumbled forward, swinging the butt of his weapon wildly into the path of the passing figure, its misaimed stock meeting only the spray from Laylan's headlong dive. Ringing axes of the work party came to a sudden stop as soldiers and locals detected the melee.

 Two Dogs squeezed the trigger sending a volley of flame and shot into the geyser of cold water raised by the dive. Across the river the small detachment of regulars, long at ease, watched indifferently from their bevies as Samuel Watson's garrison rushed to form a skirmish line.

"C'mon lads," shouted Watson, clapping his hands. The boisterous speculator-turned-Militia-Captain stood up to the glares of his uneasy neighbors, shoving them towards the noise and confusion. From across the stream came sporadic crackle of musket fire driving the little garrison pell-mell back into the shadow of the blockhouse.

"Where's my God dammed volley?" spat the Captain, jerking the tavern keeper's lapels until they were nose-to-nose. "Mr. Ogle we are a partnership are we not?" Ogle nodded uncomfortably, wincing at the sizzle of a stray round which embedded itself in the fort's clay daubing two yards from his head. "We are civic leaders you and I, are we not?" questioned Watson a second time releasing his grip on Ogle. "And, we must show for it! Now Enoch, take your polished musket out of the mud and put it to some effect."

Richard Crawford, the settlement blacksmith, understood what Watson meant. With a strong tug, he pulled his brother and two other men from their shelter as Ogle aligned his sites. "Mr. Ogle," demanded Watson once more, "I do not wish to make a game of it sir, now let's see a damned skirmish line if you please!"

"You heard the Captain," bellowed Ogle, his deep voice now eclipsed by the hasty discharge of the garrison's rifles. "We outnumber them," he shouted, pushing his men towards the shallow ford. "Shall I give chase, Sir?"

There was no answer; Watson wasn't there. Craning his neck around, Olgle found Watson's blue waist coat flung over a low-lying branch.

"The Captain's skedaddled down the embankment," stammered Crawford as he pulled the ramrod from his musket. "Enoch, Lieutenant, don't you think…"

"For God's sake Richard load your weapon," snarled Ogle, cutting short the blacksmith's thought.

From down the embankment a voice was heard through the smoke and din. It was Watson's voice hailing Laylan. "You there!" Lying in a heap and barely on the bank, Laylan slowly opened an eye and cocked an ear towards the tangled thicket above him. "You there!" repeated the voice in a more threatening tone. "If you cannot move or speak I shall leave you in the river for dead." Watson's arm probed the jumble of blackberry canes, grabbing at the stranded traveler. Another round buzzed through the tall grass, splattering the mud next to Laylan's thigh. The open hand now balled itself into a fist to better fit through the tangle. "You are making a fine target of me!" shouted Watson angrily, opening his hand once more. Laylan clenched his teeth as he extended his forearm painfully into Watson's strong grasp. Watson pulled Laylan, roughly, excruciatingly, to the Captain's feet.

"Can you move?" asked Watson, crouching down to the stranger's ear. Laylan nodded the affirmative and struggled to his knees. "Now," said Watson, "Run for it if you can manage. Don't stop until my men stop you. I'll be close behind."

Watson vanished into foliage bordering the freshly cut road, emerging seconds later with a frightened girl, who he found sheltered from the shooting behind a dying heifer. Laylan scrambled on hands and knees until he reached the chaotic scene at the militia line. The skirmish had ended.

Through the lifting smoke and dust, one-by-one, a trickle of children ran from makeshift hiding places to the arms of their anxious parents who had begun searching surrounding thickets.

Chuckles broke out at the militia regulars' encampment as the raw citizen militia congratulated each other with loud whoops and pats on the back. A few of the younger men haphazardly stacked their rifles in the shade of the blockhouse overhang and drew their skinning knives, eagerly prying leaden souvenirs from splintered blockhouse logs. Others cautiously forded the Clearfork in a half-hearted attempt to pursue the unknown force.

Mrs. McCleur pushed her way through the gathering, and wrenched her daughter's hand from Watson's, shielding the girl behind the flaps of her threadbare homespun apron.

"Thankfully, your milk cow was the only casualty today," the Captain said softly. "She can be found lying near the wagon trail. I would advise, ma'am, that it be butchered before the flies set upon it."

"This will impoverish us," said Mrs. McCleur, "and in my husband's absence, who will look after us?"

"Your husband?" retorted Watson. "Your husband should have better sense than to allow his women folk to fend for themselves."

"My husband has obligations," snapped Mrs. McCleur, "He…"

"Your husband fancies himself an itinerant judge, squatter, distiller, you name it," interrupted Watson meeting her leer. "Thinks he's the law of the land. So, tell me then; what matter of justice has drawn him from such an important post?"

"You mock us," sobbed Mrs. McCleur, turning her back to the Captain.

"I shall speak my mind when spoken-to," growled Watson as he surveyed Laylan's wounds. "That is my charge, Madame, for keeping you in milk and cheese." The traumatized and confused Mrs. McCleur had heard enough and stormed out.

"She's gone," murmured Laylan as Watson busied himself with the garrison's medicine chest. He removed a flask of laudanum and handed it to Laylan, who took a swig, his face recoiling from the bitterness.

"She'll be back," added Ogle in a lowered voice. "A poor woman as I have ever seen; an innocent as far as I am concerned. And as for McCleur, well, when the end of your circuit is a three-day ride, what is a man to do?"

"That's between Mr. McCleur and himself," glared Watson, "…and for myself, Enoch, I think I shall retreat to the hearth of your tavern. It is the only place mosquitos dare not go."

Within a dappled circle of light spilling from a single hanging lantern, Mr. Ogle honed a long, tarnished blade, placing it with his ladle and skewer on each side of a large barrel head with the fastidiousness of a trained surgeon. "Ogle," as everyone called him, a man of short stature, wasted little time in peeling onions he had pulled one-by-one from a braided strand suspended from a ceiling beam among the drying ribbons of venison and pike. Hungry young regular army officers packed themselves into the narrow room wondering eagerly what concoction the irritable tavern-keep was simmering in his blackened kettle. Watson quietly smoked a pipe in a corner which was obviously his territory. He re-read a tatter of newsprint passed along by the visiting infantry.

"I say, Enoch," shouted Watson out of the blue. "Do you recall Tom Lyons?" He folded the paper and passed it to the busy inn keeper. "According to this privy rag the old bastard ran afoul of some dragoons near the Maumee. They

found him wearing a red great coat, mind you—
says a lot for our kindred neighbors, does it not?"

"Well I suspect he'll do the hangman's jig
back in Coshocton," added Ogle, tossing the
broadside into the roaring hearth. "And his skull
will end up on the mail pole like Toby's I suppose.
"Ah well," sighed the tavern keeper palming
another onion. "I never liked him much anyway."

"Oh, I doubt that will happen, Enoch,"
replied Watson in a cloud of rising smoke. "It seems
that he, and practically every other savage in this
valley is on the Quartermaster's payroll."

"And Johnny Bulls as well," chuckled John
Oldfield, a neighbor of McCleur, as the others in the
dank tavern murmured to themselves. "I say Ogle,
did they really trice up Toby's head at Mansfield?"

"Aye they did," replied Ogle, raising an
eyebrow to Oldfield's small son now hiding under
the tavern keeper's bench. "…and when the stink
got the better of the village, the innkeeper wanted to
remove it to the crotch of that old paw-paw tree.
You know, the one by the tavern shithouse, so as to
attract enough insects for pollination—a fancy
offering to the common blow fly, eh? But his wife
made him throw it on the burn pile and be done
with it. I guess old Toby's ashes will sweeten next
year's melon patch."

"On the payroll?" muttered Laylan from his
cot.

"If Toby were an agent, the garrison at Mansfield certainly made no distinction," said the Captain. Laylan took another swig of laudanum and passed the small leather flask back to him. "I was there in the forest that day and there was no quarter given to Toby."

"Do not agonize over such things," said Watson, taking the flask. "The war for Ohio is meant to be a war of extermination, from the Maumee rapids all the way south to the Ohio River. That is what the English and their savages intend for us. If we are to have no quarter, then sir, neither shall they. I would happily fruit my paw-paws with the heads of Brits and Torys—without distinctions! And as for you, Laylan, most men of your standing desert. Hell, personally I don't blame them, not one bit. But you, sir, you by God have earned your furlough."

Across the Clear Fork, Two Dogs gathered his party as shadows deepened across the whole valley transforming its footpaths. Like processionals through vaulted corridors, cloistered with timber columns, they twisted and gradually vanished into an abyss of hellish sounds, blurry shapes, glowing eyes—and highwaymen.

"Please don't leave me to the wolves," sputtered seriously wounded Gem James, dropping to his knees. Two dogs sneered at the Irishman as he stepped over his crumpled form to allow Monsieur Light to bring a bottle to James' lips. No sooner had he swallowed than the drink oozed, red with blood, from the blackened hole in his upper chest causing James paroxysms of agony.

"I have very little use for a sieve," said Light quietly to the Wyandot. James brought himself to his knees, dropping the earthen jug and crawling to the tip of Light's boots. "Although," Light mused, "there is a place in my heart for loyal Irishmen." "Two Dogs," called Light, wiping the sweat from James' forehead, "Should we take him with us?"

"He is too heavy for the journey," whispered Two Dogs sternly.

"Well," said Light to the shaking Irishman, "I think you shall remain with us." Light daubed his brow a final time kissing James's forehead. "Bon," he said leaving James to the darkest knave of the woods.

"Now you should pray to your God," spoke Two Dogs gravely, "before I take you with me." James smiled, laboring to finish the sign of the cross, and then whispering, he began. "Our Father who art in heaven…"

Without warning the tomahawk flashed cleaving the top of James' skull. Two Dogs threw himself upon the twitching corpse with animal-like ferocity, tearing with his fingers the scalp from its bloody cap, then abandoning the Irishman's offal to the nocturnal beasts.

Thames Valley
December, 1813

Lower Canadian Frontier
"We will leave our bones in this valley…"

 A lone wagon creaking from the weight of two great casks of rancine wine groaned slowly down a thin staggered line of U. S. regulars and militia under the command of General Harrison. The inebriated server splashed rhythmically into the stoven barrels, plunging his long-handled ladle deep, slopping the foul and well-watered concoction onto clanking tins held by troops gathering below. Far across the open field droned pipes, horns and drums of the British infantry, flanked by their Native allies who were howling, hidden as yet in the blackness of surrounding swamp.

Straining to ignore the spectacle, George McCullough looked over his shoulder at the young drummer trembling at his side. "I hope you soon run out of piss lad," he said half joking, "before our boots soak through." A lone snicker followed by snorts of nervous laughter spread like an infection through his anxious men, breaking the oppressive stillness.

"Shut your trap," snapped John Gilkison, stuffing a handful of paper cartridges into McCullough's sling box. "For God's sake think of your mother, or your maker," he growled, moving to the next man. "It will do you well to say a prayer, lads," he added, bringing his column back to a hush.

Across the muddy plain, British General Procter grimaced, no longer able to bear with stoicism the prolonged ravages of fever and dysentery he had suffered. "So, this is the flower of Washington," he commented as he trained his glass on Harrison who was issuing orders to his staff officers some 600 yards ahead. "Ready the cannon," he calmly told an aid. "Take some men from my staff, unlimber it yourselves if you have to. I wish to welcome our distant cousin." Tecumseh, garbed in an officer's scarlet dress coat cantered his mount well ahead of the color guard meeting Procter within range of the American pickets. Bullets began flying.

"Assassins," muttered Procter recoiling from their hasty fusillade. "They show little distinction between officers and basic soldiery," Proctor added dryly. "In Portugal, you understand, we camped our men within musket shot of Napoleon's infantry and nary a one on either side cost a man."

Tecumseh indifferent to the subject peered intently through the glass. A wry smile began to form on his otherwise stern demeanor. "What pleases my great Chief?" asked Proctor of Bloody Eyes, Tecumseh's interpreter.

"I have known him since he was a child," replied Bloody Eyes without bothering his benefactor. "He has smiled but twice that I can recall. I have seen this during the capitulation of Fort Detroit. He did smile and said our fortunes were changing. Later we left the place barren." Bloody Eyes paused and handed Tecumseh a brace of loaded pistols. "When we returned to our camp and learned of his mother-in-law's death, again he smiled and said "Our fortunes are changing."

"Well," interrupted Proctor, raising his hand while making eye contact with his field gun crew, "This shall keep him in good spirits!" The report was deafening, followed closely by the crash of its eight-pound projectile in an explosion of wine, wood and gore as it obliterated Harrison's lone refreshment wagon.

McCullough shouted to the terrified drummer boy, "There are trees to the rear of us. As long as we advance I want you to be brave. Beat the time just as Gilkison taught you, and when we let loose the first volley, you run!" McCullough clapped his free hand on the boy's shoulder, turning him towards the swamp, its periphery now swarming with hundreds of painted warriors, fiercely keyed-up for battle. "Once you start, don't look back and don't stop for anything. This is hellish business what we have today."

"What is this about?" prodded Morrison checking the flint on his musket, "Is this little pox a relative of yours?" McCullough did not laugh. "This lad will be cut down before we will," he said pointing to a small troop of dragoons gathering at the British flanks.

"Worry about you own hide, my friend," Morrison interrupted "and let the boy alone."

"Alright, let's go!" shouted Gilkison through the blare of opposing horn calls. His column moved faster and faster, some slipping in mire churned by the teamsters. A few Kentuckians impatiently threw aside discharged muskets, drawing from their belts an array of tomahawks and knives, their rage swelling with the drummer's increasing tempo.

"My brothers, it is time," roared Tecumseh to the wolf calls and war cries of his restless Natives. He rode toward and among Proctor's field officers touching with his fingertips their shouldered sabers, repeating a Shawnee incantation. "Shall we live to make children?" he chided, turning to the 41st Glen Gary Lights now marching double-time, sending an eruption of huzzahs rippling through the scarlet ranks.

"We'll not step back my brother," swore Proctor to the Chieftain privately. "We shall mingle our bones together on this field if that's what the fates have planned. There will be no concessions." Tecumseh said nothing, vanishing with a suddenness that always annoyed the General.

"Damn them," cursed Harrison from behind the slow-moving right flank of U. S. regulars, his fists clenched, "The British will be old men by the time we reach their lines." From the opposing bluff Proctor's lone cannon kicked back violently in a cape of smoke, its double-loaded shot skipping like river stones into the mass of terrified militia advancing on the now quiet Natives laying low among the wooded thickets. Harrison held his cavalry back from the militia's flank, stopping James Johnson, commander of the mounted Kentuckians.

"You," shouted Harrison in a huff. "Richard Johnson's brother is it?"

"Yes sir," replied Johnson uncomfortably.

"Can your men overwhelm these savages before we hit the British flanks?" Harrison asked, drawing his sword.

"I will try, sir," answered the officer. Harrison repeated the question.

"I will die trying!" came the answer. Not until he asked the question a third time and got a response, "Yes sir!" did Harrison wave him off.

"Sir, a moment," thundered Richard Johnson over the objections of his older brother's subordinates. "Let me ride in place of James, he can take my posting with the riflemen."

"What's this?" protested James, eyeing his brother.

"James this task, your outfit will certainly be decimated."

"Make your decision!" shouted Harrison. "I don't give a tinker's damn who leads your horsemen. Just make it so, and make it quick!"

"James! Stop!" shouted Richard, trotting his mare to the head of the troop, blocking him from the position. "Damn it brother, you have eight children and a wife—near invalid from the experience. Our sister, God bless, is the only one keeping your house in order. Do you intend to make a spinster of her?"

"There is no honor in this!" replied James, growing flush with anger.

"Brother, I have no wife, no children that I know of. Why do you ante-up your life with so little care? The stakes are high."

"Bugler!" shouted Richard abruptly throwing down his hat. "Let us trample the red men—no quarter!" He galloped well ahead of the charging horsemen flashing a saber above his head screaming like a fiend from hell. Johnson gnashed his teeth, spurring his charger into the closing ring of warriors enveloping the Kentuckian vanguard. Never in the past did he flinch when facing a brawl or knife fight. It was only after a good scare that he pondered the terrible danger. His eyes narrowed, focusing like a diving hawk on his intended prey as they engaged. His mount bucked wildly as the warriors grew strident in their efforts to dismount him, violently slashing at the mount's kicking haunches.

"Damn you" snarled Johnson, whipping his saber overhead in a scythe-like manner, cleaving in a stroke the feathered head of a warrior who dared touch his reigns. Surprised, the scattering Shawnee responded with a murderous fire, tearing to pieces the bugler engaged not far behind. A musket ball found Johnson, forcing him to clutch his side and lean into the saddle horn as pain grew intolerable and the ground beneath him began to spin. A second well-placed shot through the wrist released his steel grip on the blade allowing it to fall away. Mad with fury and fear, Johnson's horse laid back his ears, took the bit in his teeth and reared like an enraged monster, stamping through this hailstorm of musketry and crashing into a scourge of briars hedging the great glen.

Tecumseh held a knife and pistol as he moved stealthily into the horse mottled thicket, ignoring the sizzle of flying lead that cut Bloody Eyes nearly in two.

"Don't let the Chief get away!" came a voice through the choking wall of smoke and fire. Another murderous volley ripped through the wavering Shawnee now running for their lives, completely routed.

"Proctor's left the field with his dragoons," thundered the colonel's brother, galloping through despite the demands and warnings of the rear picket.

"Where is your colonel?" he shouted, scanning the line of skirmishers now firing at their will.

"Oh, Colonel Johnson? Poor bastard fell in them briars..." answered a wounded Kentuckian propped up against a riddled log. "Dead I am afraid."

"Dear God Richard, what have you done!" cried James as he dismounted. "Richard, Richard you bastard!" he shouted repeatedly, his voice carrying off into the mire until, as if by Providence, the horse's trail revealed itself through a sulfurous veil of burnt powder.

Deftly, Tecumseh followed the blood-slicked trail, moving serpent-like towards the Colonel, now struggling beneath his dying mount. Johnson loosened a long horse pistol loaded with buck-and-ball while his horse thrashed about in a futile effort to right itself, crushing the Colonel's pinned knee. Johnson cried out from the pain, then raised the long barrel to his right temple whispering the Lord's Prayer.

"How will God receive me?" he thought as he pondered the great sin, pulling the firelock with his thumb and forefinger to full cock. Suddenly, the beast jerked again, raising its ears to the sound of moccasins quickening their pace. Johnson squinted into the sun focusing on the path's narrow opening. "I'll take this savage straight to hell with me," thought Johnson with a macabre sense of relief. "At least my scalp will not become a trophy."

Tecumseh tightened his grip on the knife, drew a deep breath as his eyes met those of his quarry, and in an instant he was on Johnson's recumbent body, driving the knife into his shoulder joint separating it with a twist. Johnson screamed nearly dropping the pistol as he leveled the barrel just over his head, jerking the trigger against the chieftain's blurry silhouette which disappeared in the shower of sparks and flame. Johnson closed his eyes, lacking strength for further resistance, waiting for the coup-de-grace which was sure to come at the hands of an enraged warrior. There was a dreadful pause as the twisting knife stopped and Tecumseh collapsed with a thud into the trampled sedges beside him.

Soon the frenzied crackle of back-and-forth volleys dwindled to a few celebratory shots followed by the huzzahs of Harrison's regulars now occupying Proctor's encampment, stripping it of much needed supplies.

"You there, McCullough!" shouted Gilkison through the rising din of fortunate men, their laughter forming a bizarre duet with the cries of the dying. "McCullough is that you Goddammit!" Gilkison repressed the urge to vomit from the hellish scene.

"I am not deaf," came the answer with much annoyance. "Can't you see I'm busy." McCullough scraped his knife across the ashen crown of a dead Shawnee, ripping and tearing back the scalp with a force that required no further cut. Gilkison watched in disgust as McCullough tossed the scalp onto a mounting pile beside the row of dead warriors.

"Alive and well, I see," replied the Sergeant taking the roll. "And what of Morrison? Where can he be found? Gilkison stood over McCullough, resisting the urge to kick the man as he was kept waiting.

"Well, Sir," began McCullough slowly "I lost track of the pudding-head in Proctor's baggage train. "Turns out our drummer found stacks of deeds for land around the big swamp, confiscated from General Hull two years back. Morrison gave the boy his pay for some of them damn papers."

"What!" cried Gilkison, grabbing him by the collar so that they stood eye-to-eye. "Please continue."

"Well," coughed McCullough, "Well then Morrison found the General's steward—a French bastard hiding in the dunnage—and after a box to the ears, he told George that His Lordship had been using them as legal tender, paying them to his victualers and spies."

"And Morrison?" growled Gilkison.

"Took French leave Sir, at least that's what the boys call it," smiled McCullough, "Gives it an air of legitimacy."

Ten feet away, cavalrymen took their ease with pilfered rum as they gawked at a skinned cadaver which was being towed by a rope behind the Major's snorting charger.

"They say that's Tecumseh," said McCullough as he bit off a plug of tobacco. "Damned near killed Colonel Johnson in them weeds, but the Colonel did for him, and then some." McCullough spat, wiping the dribble on his waistcoat. "Well at any rate I made a fine strop of old Tecumseh's backside. No sir, a better morning could not be had."

Gilkison frowned and turned his back on McCullough. He raised a bottle thrust into his hand by some subordinate. The swamp, the dead, the clear blue sky—it all seemed so vivid and yet unreal. He took a long pull from the bottle and searched among the bodies for the firebrand Kanotchy. He did not see him fall. Perhaps he imagined it. Maybe Kanotchy was never there at all. Gilkison dropped the bottle and rubbed his eyes, hoping for clarity. It was clear he was in command due to the injuries of his superiors who had lead the charge. Sharply, he drew his men up into a long line two abreast and slowly marched them (herded them really) out of the mire, with Johnson and most of his staff floating on stretchers shouldered by more able men.

The Hunt

Calvin Culver raised his musket but saw nothing as he sighted down the barrel and off into the dark looming tree line. Slowly he laid back down into the sumac tangle, perfectly immobile, until he heard the usual noises of birds, insects and frogs return. But everything was not quite normal. His nose detected a strange earthy smell, barely detectable above the normal fragrances of blooming plants. "Oh God no!" he cursed as a large bruin charged through the mist knocking him back into the bushes. His neighbor Tom Arbuckle, stationed behind a nearby log, heard the cries of human agony.

"Mr. Gilkison, I was so scared I couldn't move; I couldn't even rouse the dogs." reported Arbuckle in a hushed tone so no one else in the tavern could hear the tale.

"Don't beat yourself up over it," consoled Gilkison as he returned his pencil and tablet to a desk drawer that, along with his printing press, now occupied a draped-off corner of Williams Tavern. This rented space now served as Gilkison's newspaper office. "My father used to say 'There are bears and then there are bears.'" mused the editor of the *Olive*.

Outside the curtain, Mr. Culver lay on an adjacent table immobilized by excruciating pain, his abdomen bound tightly in Linsey bandages.

"Mr. Culver took a nasty swipe to the gut." commented Elizabeth Gilkison using a goose quill to scrape dried ink from the worn brass type, replacing one block for another on the wrought iron set rack. "Should you not prepare your readers for the worst? He can't possibly live…"

"He'll pull through." said Gilkison, pouring Arbuckle another drink. "I've seen lads with more wicked wounds survive." And indeed he had, during his years in the military. "I do not wish to nail Mr. Culver into his coffin prematurely. Of course, if one guides this in the right direction, it could be advantageous to the township."

"Grand Hunt to be Held," read George Coffinberry at breakfast the next morning. "By the Gods, is this what you call a headline, John?" he smirked taking the latest issue of The *Olive* from his wife with a kiss. "A grand hunt? That will not cure Culver's stomach ache. Do you remember the last 'grand hunt?' By my estimation half of the hogs in the township went missing."

"You're missing the point." said Gilkison who was immune to Coffinberry's criticism. "Soon your tenants will be flush with the silver from visiting hunters, a rare commodity in these parts. They will pay their rent in specie instead of whiskey or notes of faith."

"One hunt will do all of that?" Coffinberry smiled and wiped egg yolk from his whiskers. A rip to the gut and you devise a scheme to bring-in outside money while eliminating a risk to our common well-being—the power of the press, eh? My advice would be to let politicians worry about the economy and leave speculation about Mr. Culver's health to his physician."

A week had passed before the Eve of the hunt when, in crisp twilight, fifty or more hunters gathered at a bonfire in the center of town. Winship kindled it fearing they would strip his garden fence in order to warm themselves. Around the square, shutters closed as rowdy drunks fired guns into the sky, the lead falling like hailstones on clapboard roofs and brick chimneys of homes, which had proliferated year-by-year near the commons. Spirits were high going into the hunt. Six large wolves had been killed two days before on the road to Lexington, their severed heads now displayed as trophies in the window of E. P. Sturges's general store.

By sunrise the next morning, a pack of hunters concealed themselves in underbrush surrounding the great spring, a watering hole frequented by animals that roamed nearby groves of Chestnut and Beech. A rutted path of hard-packed earth lead to the water's edge, its grooved shape formed in millennia past, by once great herds of thirsty bison. For an hour or so they listened as an enormous bear approached his sow who was guarding her offspring as they drank. With a drop of his hand the hunting party's leader unleashed the eager men, some of whom leapt to their feet yelling savage war cries revived from distant memories, as others unleashed a deadly hail of shot and flame. This execution squad reloaded as the wounded animals thrashed around, turning the spring red. They fired a second volley into the bruin, who had shaken-off his wounds from the first and was reeling like a ritual dancer by the now lifeless pack.

 Again they fired until the dance was over. When deemed safe, the men went to work with knives, taking only claws and teeth for souvenirs while the dogs strained for their turn at the spoils and birds fled from trees in the forest to the chimneys and spires of town, avoiding the cacophony.

1846

A steam engine roared across the countryside, once dense forest, now plowed and harrowed for cultivation. Onlookers gazed in awe at the spectacle of this machine. From its narrow smokestack spat soot and embers onto a dampened tarpaulin awning that covered its few jostled passengers who were on a recruiting tour for the Mexican War. They sat precariously on benches bolted to a flat car. The *"Empire,"* as the Sandusky-Newark engineers called it, dipped and rattled its way over the bridge at Toby's Run toward the city, just as the sun became entangled in the trees that cradled the uneven tracks. The bridge, a pole trestle, was no level affair, its sagging unseasoned timbers straining against pinned iron straps causing the whole span to yaw when met by Empire's unbalanced mass.

"City of Mansfield one mile ahead!" shouted a mechanic over the loud banging engine. "Oh, the coach stands rotting in the yard. The horse has sought the plow." bellowed the engineer between blasts of the steam whistle.

"That man is drunk." shouted Winn Winship, trying not to move from his cramped place on the bench. "This flammable contraption lacks even a cow catcher up forward, you see," pointing outward with his cane. "Truly reckless it is!" he groused to no one in particular. Winship's son-in-law, James, looked at his pocket watch and frowned, the third time he did so in the last five minutes.

"These locomotive engines are a spot different in Pittsburgh, I dare say," complained the gout-ridden Winship, adding irritation to James's overall discomfort. "Lord, can't they navigate this toy in a calmer fashion?" In between the two men, Richard Johnson kept to his cot, a narrow assemblage of skins that had been slung below stanchions for the great hero's comfort.

"Have I told you, James…" began Winship, interrupting Johnson's thoughts. "You see, young man, it was not fifty years ago that myself, our Captain Johnson, James Kinney and a few others cleared the first trees in Mansfield proper—by God we lived like animals then."

"We've all heard the story, Winn," growled Johnson taking a medicinal swig from a large jug that the chief mechanic had sent aft to bolster their constitutions. Johnson smiled as the liquid they called "honey dew" swept him up in a sudden warmth which he appreciated more with each passing mile. A day had gone by since he boarded in Sandusky and had been steadfastly temperant, refusing the jug as Winship did at each go-round. It was Plymouth that turned his resolve. "Damn Plymouth," he said as he took another sip "and damn my aching back!" It was not the place that stoked his ire, but a tow path that engineers called the Plymouth gap. It was a finger of boggy swamp south of town where a team of draft horses pulled the engine and cars through submersed tracks and onto drier undulating ground of Richland County. Before this ordeal he moved about with an ease that surprised those who had remembered the severity of his wounds at Thames. This seemingly normal movement was a bit of theatre that he used to conceal his constant pain. Only now was he coming to doubt his ability to move off the cot.

The steam whistle blasted out its call in three successive shrill blasts as the engine slowed to the huzzahs of various militia companies awaiting

embarkation to the plains of Mexico to fight the new war there. James loosened his frock revealing an ill-fitting blue officer's uniform from a bygone time.

"Be sure to keep your commission with you at all times!" warned Winship as he adjusted the young man's epaulets. "And do not forget the goggles I procured for you. Mexican territory, I am told, is a bilious place of sand and grit."

"Rumpsey Dumpsy," shouted a recruit, then another joined in as the train jolted to its final stop.

"What does it mean?" asked James craning his neck at the growing crowd. Johnson frowned. The crowd, now fifty strong, began chanting a little jingle:

"Rumpsey Dumpsey

Rumpsey Dumpsey

Richard Johnson killed Tecumseh."

"Ah yes, now I remember," mused Winship. "The crowds first took to it back in '36 when Mr. Johnson here, became Vice President under Van Buren, as you recall. Beat out old Harrison, you see—ha ha ha. As it happens there was no shortage of men who, after going to war with Johnson, did not come out either dead or a politician—ha—and there's the truth of it."

"Is it true what the crowd is saying?" asked James who was helping Johnson to his feet.

"So they say," shrugged Johnson waving to the mob.

Through the streets and across the front yards of ramshackle houses came more recruits and well-wishers, flowing with gathering speed down the main avenue, mesmerized by the shrill blast of *Empire's* whistle. The train came to a stop at the more gentrified Walnut Street platform, within sight of John Gilkison's house.

"Rabble," puffed Gilkison. His nose almost pressed against the drawing room window. "Children are playing soldier."

"Please try to relax," said his son, Mansfield Gilkison, speaking for the first time since entering the room. "Dr. Bushnell worries for your heart. He believes your humors are in ill form."

"Hogwash!" he replied. "By God, who gave them uniforms? The lot of them are as confused as our President. And Mexico—a more immoral conquest could not be had. But alas Mr. Polk needs a sideshow!" Gilkison's ears perked to the sound of water boiling away inside the Japaned pot on the brazier at the other end of the room. "Well son, at least there is the bean—coffee with you?"

"No thank you." said Mansfield as he went for the paper. "You should quit that stuff. I believe it only makes you cross." Gilkison waved him off, pouring the grounds into boiling water and setting it aside to steep, its aroma eroding his black mood.

"Is not Polk's war declaration a mere continuance of the principles that lead to war in 1812?" asked Mansfield as he sat down into an easy chair. "Is this not manifest destiny? At least that is the opinion of Richard Johnson. It's here in the paper."

The aging newsman's eyebrows came together. "Manifest destiny? Is that how he puts it? That term did not exist in the summer of Twelve. No, we did not give a damn for Canada or sailor's rights or Mr. Madison's war. We worried for our scalps, you see. Not everyone prospered as Mr. Johnson or I did in its aftermath. Count yourself lucky to have never seen a severed head thrust upon a pole in the commons." Gilkison sighed as he poured a cup of cold water into the pot, allowing the grounds to settle.

"Mr. Johnson is about to speak." said Mansfield, moving to his father's side by the window. "If you wish to hear it, I could open the transom."

"No, I've heard this story a time or two before."

Notes

Prologue

Mansfield's current site was not the expected choice for the soon-to-be settlement. Early land speculator and surveyor Jacob Newman built a cabin and saw mill at a site on the Rocky Fork *(R. A. Carter 2016, 166)*, which, with the addition of a grist mill, became known as Beam's mill (near what is now State Route 39 and Mount Zion Road). This location never became a town for lack of clean water (other than well water) which surveyors discovered was lavished on a broad, spring-fed hummock a few miles away, that we know today as downtown Mansfield. Early trappers, traders and surveyors often took temporary shelter in large hollow trees when passing through the wilderness. Chapman found Peter Kinney living in a tree when he went to the rendezvous described in the prologue (Duff *1931, 79*). These early surveyors and scouts included names familiar to Mansfield residents today: Jacob Newman, John Chapman, James Hedges, Joseph Larwill, George Coffinberry, Winn Winship and John Gilkison (*Graham* 1880, 449).

Brownstown Creek

The threat of frontier violence in central Ohio during the war of 1812, and the panic that sometimes ensued, had its roots in General Hull's brief and disastrous invasion of upper Canada during July of 1812. There, outside of Sandwich, Hull's Ohio and Kentucky volunteers stripped the surrounding countryside of livestock, produce and forage, famishing and alienating the very populace that Hull had promised to protect against the many depredations of the British-lead Indian tribes. Ironically, the British crown had sworn to protect Canada's southernmost inhabitants from the same threat.

Foodstuffs became scarce on both sides as Hull's line of supplies, promised by the government in Washington, never materialized, dooming Hull's invasion before it ever got going. British soldiers, like their American counterparts deserted in droves, starved by the inability of the British provincial government to provide vast amounts of rations and tributes demanded by Tecumseh's confederation. Supplies that the warriors did not take, they burned to keep them out of American hands. This drove both sides into a struggle more for survival than for liberation or loyalty. Fear and hatred of tribal warriors pouring into the region terrified Hull's men. Even the British marching alongside them were intimidated.

The pot boiled over when, during the battle of Amhurstburg on July 15, 1812. William McCullough, an officer in Hull's Ohio militia, killed and scalped a Menominee chieftain after seizing the main bridge north of town. Inexplicably, Hull ordered a withdrawal, turning a near victory into a disastrous defeat. The Canadians and British drove him out of Canada.

Incensed, the Menominee carried their dead and mutilated chieftain back to Amhurstburg, dropping him at the feet of British officers, who were savoring their turn of luck. Leaderless and enraged, the Menominee, who like most of the confederation had honored a British request not to scalp any of Hull's men, confronted the officers and vowed to resume the scalping of their enemies *(Taylor 2010, 210)*.

Indians saw dark humor when white settlers rebuked them for scalping. James Commons, a sergeant in the British army at Amhurstburg found this hypocrisy intolerable. He wrote of the Ohio and Kentucky militia: "They are served out with blanket clothing like the Indians, with a long scalloping [sic] knife and other barbarous articles and red paint with which they daub themselves all over. And in the summer time go about naked. In this manner, they would surprise our piquets and, after engagements, would scallop [sic] the killed and wounded that could not get out of the way *(Taylor 2010, 208)*."

In June, 1812, Major Thomas Van Horne, commanding, a party of Ohio Militia 200 strong, crossed Brownstown Creek just south of the river Raisin, near present-day Gibralter, Michigan. Ambushed by Tecumseh's Shawnee and Wyandot warriors, the militia, most of them young recruits, fled before the painted braves, a war party numbering only twenty. In less than an hour, 18 Ohio riflemen lay dead on the creek's broad flood plain. William McCullough was one of them. Only twelve reported back to Fort Detroit. The fallen were scalped and many were impaled on stakes along the trial to Detroit *(Berton 1980, 159)*. The rest of Van Horne's command, not to the surprise of Hull, deserted back to their homesteads in Central Ohio.

The cause of the ambush, ironically, was revenge for the killing of the chieftain by William McCullough, Samuel's older brother, who displayed the chief's scalp as an ornament on his saddle.

During the war of 1812 (and indeed much later) an officer's commission in the regular army could be bought outright or given as a favor by political patronage. Remarkably, unlike the Navy, no form of training or experience was required. Hull, at 63 was the exception, being part of a small aging nucleus of career officers, battle-tested in the Revolutionary War thirty years before. The General, along with Ethan Allen and Benedict Arnold had turned the tide at the Battle of Saratoga, becoming one of General Washington's favorite field commanders both during and after the war.

As a stipulation for his governorship of Detroit and the march on upper Canada, Hull demanded and was promised an army comprised of regular soldiers and officers, with the Ohio and Kentucky militia in a limited role as skirmishers.

He soon found out that a professional army, as well as the supplies necessary for success never materialized. General Hull's officers and men were mainly homesteaders from the Ohio and Kentucky wilderness. It was their rough and violent demeanor, which appalled Detroit's French-speaking inhabitants and inflamed the tribes, that so unnerved the General.

A few, like William McCullough, found themselves marching in a force greatly reduced, both in numbers and in quality, into a battle that Hull, on the verge of victory, found unwinnable. This turnaround sealed his fate, because it served as justification for the mutinous behavior of his politician-turned-militia officers, grumbling at Fort Detroit.

General Hull had a lot on his mind in the summer of 1812. He was openly hated by his men and all but ostracized by other militia officers, whom he denounced in letters as mutinous cowards and bandits (*Taylor* 2010, 162), He became racked by nightmares and incapacitated by sickness as he languished in his quarters at Fort Detroit. He had been receiving reports, almost daily, of Tecumseh's push to unite the tribes of Ohio and lower Michigan with the Shawnee confederacy, in their bid to reclaim the region from American land speculators and the tenuous hold of the U. S. Military. The other chiefs listened as the Shawnee supported a promise by the British to join them and overrun the Ohio frontier, creating a dead zone from the shores of Lake Erie to the banks of the Ohio River. This land would revert to an aboriginal state supplied exclusively by British trade. In the chaos that ensued, Indians found alone were often shot on sight, a fact confirmed by aging pioneers in their letters and memoirs. A man named Mortimer, writing soon after the Greentown removal, spoke of the growing threat of violence facing local tribes as war loomed. In an excerpt from a letter dated August 10, 1812, he recalled: "Many declair that if they saw any strange Indian they would shoot him. I have even been assured by the most credible persons, that some have asserted openly—possibly while intoxicated—that they would have killed every Indian here (Greentown) before they left their families and marched with the militia, and the persons who gave me this information have repeatedly added, that they beleave [sic] this to be the prevailing sentiment in this country *(Neel* 2009, 13)."

After closing the proceedings against Van Horne, General Hull collapsed at his desk, suffering a series of strokes that enfeebled him. He had long ignored a heart condition in order to take the opportunity to govern the Michigan Territory.

As Hull grew weaker, his militia officers squabbled over their rank and personal honor, most of them refusing, at first, to cross the Canadian border, citing at the last minute their constitutional obligation to stay within the United States frontier.

Within a week of the Van Horne hearing a young Lieutenant, Porter Hanks, surrendered Fort

Michillimackinak without a shot being fired, giving British General Isaac Brock and Tecumseh a stranglehold on the region. Among the spoils were the contents of a schooner containing papers in which General Hull outlined his general orders, strategic placements, concerns and weaknesses (in his own hand). Brock and Tecumseh moved to attack Fort Detroit. When Hull declined terms of surrender, Brock fired an artillery round through the roof of the officer's barracks, splattering Hull and his daughter with the brains of young Porter Hanks. Between cannonade rounds they could hear war whoops from Tecumseh's warriors outside. After a brief artillery duel, Hull surrendered. Van Horne broke his sword rather than surrender it to the British (*Harbaugh* 1909, 134). The surrender set off a chain reaction that led to tragic events throughout the original borders of Richland County.

By the time militiamen from Richland County reached Fort Detroit, it had already fallen to the British and they were obliged to surrender. The British paroled them and sent them home. After the war Hull was court martialed and sentenced to be shot. Madison, having reviewed Hull's past exploits at Saratoga, commuted the sentence. Hull was dismissed from the military.

After August of 1812, troops poured into Mansfield from neighboring parts of the state. Many of them were veterans of Brownstown and Fort Detroit. John Gilkison's placement at Detroit is fiction (as far as I know), although it would have befitted his rank at the time to be traveling to such places. Morrison and McCullough could be counted among the inrush of troops into Richland County.

Greentown

When the earliest settlers erected their crude wilderness cabins, there was a Native American village called Greentown, established in the 1780s, in what is now Ashland County between Lucas and Perrysville, just off State Route 39. Founded by Thomas Green, a British Tory, and Chief Thomas Armstrong, an adopted brother, it was the largest village around. It was populated by 300 inhabitants--eight times the size of Mansfield. They were a mixture of displaced and defeated members of various tribes, mostly Delaware (Lenape), with some Mingos. Mowhawks and Mohegens (*Greentown Preservation Association 2018, Homepage*). Its economic base was agricultural supplemented by hunting and fishing.

Early settlers lived in accord with Greentown Indians, cooperating in trade and mutual interests. But there were growing tensions inherent in conflicts of the day. Early in the Summer of 1812, Tecumseh's emissary visited Greentown where he met with Armstrong, trying to persuade him to join Tecumseh's confederation in the coming war against the settlements. Armstrong refused, citing as a basis of his neutrality the treaty he had signed with the U. S. Government after the disastrous Battle of Fallen Timbers a decade earlier (*Levison 1908, 27*). This alienated him from Tecumseh's sphere, and peaked the distrust of local militia Captains for failing to restrict the flow of British goods into the village. Once plans of Tecumseh's confederation were made known, fears began to spread because of Greentown's proximity to Mansfield. This gave Captain Douglass the pretext he needed to forcibly remove the Delaware to reservations in Piqua and Upper Sandusky.

The captive Delaware were marched from Greentown to a ravine at the edge of Mansfield commons near a tanner's yard down the hill from what is now St. Peters Sports Center on what is now Ritter's Run. There, they spent the night in the fetid air before being marched out of the county.

Mansfield

Samuel Martin was Mansfield's first merchant, selling goods to pioneers and Greentown residents from a cabin that stood where the Reeds building is now. Soon after setting up shop, Martin was accused of selling alcohol to the Delaware, a crime that got him banished from the county. Levi Jones took his place in 1810, residing with Winn Winship in the loft of a lean-to built onto the back of the store. One year later, Winship built the first frame house, an anomaly for the area, just off the South side of the square behind Williams Tavern.

Toby was reportedly a well-liked regular visitor to Mansfield. He was known for his skill with medicinal herbs and was part of the local color, like Chapman. His death was lamented by those who knew him. Victorian historians who otherwise took a dim view of Native people, eulogized him to some extent. It was said that for years his ribs could be seen sticking out of the creek bank where he fell, possibly covered now by the bike trail. Morrison and McCullough piked Toby's severed head atop a pole on Mansfield's commons, which at the time was a muddy two-acre encampment being used by Colonel Kratzer's militia soon after General Hull's surrender of Fort Detroit. Graham states that McCullough "had fashioned a cup from Toby's scalp, in which he took his whiskey. *(Graham 1880, 275-276)*

Odyssey

We do not know the name of Toby's daughter. I have given her the name Olena, a popular pet name among Delaware girls *(Moorehead 1899, 80)*.

According to John Chapman, Toby's daughter reached Upper Sandusky eight days after the murder of her father, subsisting on blackberries and water *(R. A. Carter, Tom Lyons The Indian Who Died 13 Times 2011)*. Diarists of the day paint a dark picture of the unbroken wilderness engulfing the cabins and wigwams of early Richland County *(Knapp 1863, 17)*. Wolves gathered at the edges of beaten paths encircling those moving about at night without a lantern. Rattlesnakes were numerous, 36 being killed alone by the garrison at Mansfield after a thunderstorm drove them from their dens onto the higher ground of the square. *(R. A. Carter, Tom*

Lyons The Indian Who Died 13 Times 2011, 39). Bears made off with pigs and killed the dogs that guarded them. The local Delaware much preferred these bears to the pigs, claiming their flesh was sweet. They made a corn gruel with it that was infamously distasteful to the palates of their white dinner guests *(Taylor 2010)*. Passenger Pigeons amassed in flocks numbering in the millions, darkening the skies of Oho until hunted to extinction by the twentieth century.

The water table was much higher in pioneer times. Before the impoundments and damings of the last 150 years, the average depth of the Mohican was three feet higher than the modern mean depth. *(Trautman 1981, 15)*. Giant fish such as sturgeon, pike and gar packed even the smaller streams on their mating runs. A friend of this author possesses a wrought iron trident made by his great grandfather for spearing these monsters in the Cedar Fork near his farm. Along the Rocky Fork, *(Shea 1886)* pike weighing up to 50 pounds were shot by Delaware hunters when game could not be found.

When French traders ventured into the area, they did so by canoe, finding the waterways well maintained by Natives who relied on the streams' navigability. Many early roads followed ancient hunting trails, some of which were long-used animal paths *(G. W. Hill 1880, 35)*. Much of what is now State Route 61 was a trail pounded out by migrating bison herds over millennia. It was a logical progression from animal path, to hunting trail, to modern road. Olena would not have had to bushwhack all the way to Upper Sandusky. She would have used animal trails and creeks, yet it took eight days. Her survival skills—the ability to feed herself, navigate and avoid predators—were remarkable.

Levi Jones

There has been much confusion in modern times about the date of the murder of Levi Jones, even though historical sources are much clearer. A. A. Graham states that "...about the same time as the Indians were removed from Greentown, Levi Jones was killed near Mansfield on the 13th of August 1812 *(Graham 1880, 276)*." Graham continues "Jones was shot, stabbed and scalped by two Indians with whom he had bad dealings. This occurred at the foot of the hill on the East side on North Main Street." When the alarm was raised it was also assumed that two other men, Reed and Wallace, who went missing after working at the nearby brickyard, had been carried off by Indians or murdered as well. Frantic wives of the missing men begged Chapman to make a run to Mount Vernon for help. The local militia were not here, because they were accompanying the Greentown Delaware to Piqua. This fixes the date of Levi Jones's murder to that of the Greentown evacuation. Graham continues: "Shortly after Johnny left, Reed and Wallace made their appearance safe and sound to the great joy of all. When the soldiers arrived the next morning, the body of Levi Jones was brought in on a sled and buried, and a search was conducted for any savages that might be lurking about."

During the Spring of 1840, the Ohio historian and illustrator Henry Howe, traveled to Mansfield to interview John Gilkison, Henry Hedges, Dr. Bushnell and others about the events that took place thirty-six years before. Howe does not list sources in the modern sense, but casually mentions their meetings. If one reads the article in its entirety, *(Howe, V2)* he refers to, and quotes Gilkison directly, implying the information came from the lips of Gilkison himself: "Mr. Levi Jones was shot by some Greentown Indians in the northern part of Mansfield early in the war, somewhere near the site of Rilyes Mill. He kept a store in Mansfield, and when the Greentown Indians left, refused to give up some rifles they had left as security for debt. He was waylayed, and shot and scalped. The report of rifles being heard from town, a party went out and found his body much mutilated, and buried him in the old grave yard [*corner of First and Adams Streets*]."

Towards the end of the chapter Howe summarizes: "The murder of Jones must have happened a few days before the removal of the Greentown Indians (at Mansfield)—as at that time soldiers were already occupying the blockhouse on the square. Two weeks after the removal of the Greentown Indians, Martin Ruffner and the Zimmer family living on the Blackfork were murdered."

This places the Jones murder earlier than the Ruffner and Zimmer murders. Ruffner and Zimmer were murdered during September of 1812

A. J. Baughman supports this time frame with a letter written by a settler name Peter Hout: "In 1812 when the Indians were being removed from Greentown to Piqua, and while temporarily encamped at Mansfield, an Indian named Toby escaped, but was captured and killed near where the Leesville-West Fourth Street Road crosses the stream named for the Indian. A month or two later, Levi Jones was killed by the Indians *(Baughman 1908, 260)*

Amariah Watson *(R. A. Carter, Tom Lyons The Indian Who Died 13 Times 2011, 26-28)* in his recollections says that the inciting incident for the local murders was General Hull's surrender of Fort Detroit. and the uncertainty which followed: "After Hull's surrender and the Indians having killed our neighbor Jones, we assisted in building a fort and blockhouse on the ground where the town of Bellville is, under the command of Samuel Watson. At the time that Jones was killed the whole country fled in confusion to the settlement south (Bellville). We moved our wives, children and cattle to this settlement south. From the time of the murder of Jones to the Victory of Capt. Perry on Lake Erie, we were continuously on the scout or on guard or in fort or on alert some way from the summer of 1812 until September 1813." Watson also recalled Chapman coming to his door shouting "Jones, Wallace and Reed had been killed by the Indians, heading south" This gives us part of a route for Chapman's run being past the Watson place near Lexington.

Price offers a motive for the Jones murder: "Later the story was told that Jones had incurred the anger of several Greentown Indians by having refused, when they were moved, to return to them some rifles that they had left as security for trading post debts." This would put the murder and Chapman's run in 1812 *(Price 1967, 93)*.

Further evidence of the 1812 date come from Jones's death notice posted in the Ohio Register on August 10, 1812 *(Ohio Register 1812)*. The only remaining question is the exact day of the murder. It is easy to see why a notice of the settling of Jones's estate in 1813 would be confused for the date of the murder. The common thread running through all of the tales, which validates the 1812 date is that the militia encamped at Mansfield was removing the Greentown Indians at the time, and that was 1812. Jones's name remains as an official on public records into 1813, that is, until a successor could replace him. Government functions were disrupted by the events of the summer of 1812. People were displaced to blockhouses, and militia Colonels were temporarily in charge until Perry's victory in 1813, after which the focus of the war shifted to the frontier boundaries of New York and Upper Canada.

Efforts were made to capture Jones's murderers, who according to Margaret

Cunningham, were Quilipetoxe and Seneca John *(Cunningham 1873)*. A place where they tied their horses was found at what today is the corner of Prospect and South Main Streets. The next day a company of fifteen volunteers was organized and followed the trail to Upper Sandusky. They came so close to the fugitives on the second day that they found their campfire still burning. But a few days later these men from Mount Vernon straggled back into Mansfield empty handed. Women shuttered their doors as soldiers, stripped to the waist and painted like a Delaware war party, arrived. Some imbibed at Williams Tavern while others amused themselves discharging weapons in the air before leaving the settlement. Mansfielders were gripped with the same fears they had during Chapman's run.

Some time later, Quilipetoxe and Seneca John reappeared in Mansfield apparently unaware that their feud with Jones was well known to the townspeople. The two showed up one night at Williams Tavern brazenly wearing articles of Jones's clothing and carrying a purse full of coins. A scalp could be exchanged for four dollars at Fort Malden during the summer of 1812. They attempted to buy a large jug of whiskey. Soon an altercation developed into a brawl that spilled into the street. Seneca John and Quilipetoxe ran for their lives pursued by a mob of Jones's neighbors, until they were overtaken at a swamp, two miles from town. They were murdered, scalped and buried in the mud of the lowlands. Today this site can be seen from Illinois Avenue between the wastewater plant and Madison East Elementary School.

Decades after the war of 1812, Seneca John and Quililpetoxe were reincarnated as boogey men by mothers living in the area, to keep their children in their beds at night. To this day people refer to the site as "Spooks Hollow."

Copus, Ruffner, Zimmer

Early on the morning of September 10, 1812, Levi Bargahiser, one of Martin Ruffner's field hands, was approached by Indians from Piqua on the road to Mifflin *(Graham 1880, 877)*. They asked if Reverend Copus or Frederick Zimmer were about, and explained that Captain Douglas had given them permission to return and harvest acres of ripening corn left behind during the removal. Friendly inquiries soon turned sour as Bargahiser, noticing the Indians were armed to the teeth, began stalling. Impatient, the Indians disappeared into the wilderness headed in the direction of Zimmer's homestead.

When Martin Ruffner returned home and heard Levi's story, he grabbed his rifle, horn and shot pouch and dashed across his partially harvested field for Frederick Zimmer's cabin and encountered Philip Zimmer, Frederick's son, along the way. He sent Philip to Reverend Copus's cabin to warn him of the encounter. Copus grabbed his weapons and headed for the Zimmer place with Philip Zimmer *(Brinkerhoff 1993, 106-110)*.

Kate Zimmer, Frederick Zimmer's daughter, opened the door as was the custom, nervously welcoming Kanotchy and other warriors to the table. She prepared a meal for them as her parents no doubt kept a watchful eye. Before their removal from Greentown, some Delaware had accused Frederick Zimmer of tying clapboards to a pony's tail and lighting them on fire. He did this to express frustration because they ignored many requests to restrain the animal, which was grazing his crops. What happened next was slaughter. Young Katie was brained with a tomahawk and scalped along with her parents in short order. As the attackers prepared to burn down the cabin, Martin Ruffner arrived and jumped into the fray, shooting the first warrior he saw, and clubbing a second with his rifle before being overwhelmed and scalped *(Duff 1931, 81-82)*.

Copus and Phillip Zimmer arrived soon afterwards, narrowly escaping a similar fate. Copus along with his family and neighbors sought the safety of Beam's blockhouse and other fortified outposts. News of the Zimmer and Ruffner killings rekindled latent fears of Tecumseh's uprising. Four days later the Copus's returned home to harvest their crops, believing themselves to be safe through their friendship with Armstrong. It was also the start of the Green Corn festival when, by tradition, all conflicts and grudges were temporarily suspended *(Moorehead 1899, 286)*.

Escorting them was a detachment of nine soldiers. When morning came three of them, John Tedrick, George Shipley and William Warnock were ambushed and killed at a spring near Copus's cabin. Apparently they were washing for breakfast, their guns stacked uselessly against Copus's barn. One wounded soldier made it to the threshold of Copus's cabin through a hail of gunfire which mortally wounded Copus as he opened the door. While he lay dying in bed, his family defended their besieged cabin for five grueling hours until Kanotchy and his followers retreated with their dead. Along the way they burned the vacated cabins of Newell, Cuppy and Fry, all of whom were known for mistreating local Natives. Later in life Tom Lyons would confess to Amy Copus that he was present during the attack, but denied participating in it, and regretted the death of her husband *(R. A. Carter, Tom Lyons The Indian Who Died 13 Times 2011, 46)*. Lyons earlier told John Coltier, a neighbor of Copus who had been friendly with the Natives, that they had considered stopping at his home for a meal but worried their visit might terrify his family.

Laylan's Journey

Whether through incompetence, treachery or absolute necessity, when General Hull surrendered Fort Detroit he allowed a vast military stockpile to fall into General Brock's lap without the British suffering a single casualty. Tecumseh and the confederating tribes were jubilant, now referring to their once precarious British allies as "nitchies" or brother-friends.

Months earlier, Mansfield settlement watched as the bulk of these assets streamed north through town. People were assured by militia commanders that these supplies would be used to defend them and extend the frontier into Michigan. This would end designs on the region by the British and Tecumseh. Many local men enlisted or were conscripted, taking up arms and marching to Fort Detroit. So confident they were of turning Detroit into a military bastion that Captain Newell of Mount Vernon drew a line across what was then Richland County, allowing an exemption from conscription to those living south of Troy Township *(R. A. Carter, Tom Lyons The Indian Who Died 13 Times 2011, 26).* During this period military provisions were easily obtained and were parceled-out for self-protection to nervous homesteaders as a substitute for the men conscripted from their households. The idea was to make them able to defend themselves against growing threats from Indians.

Amariah Watson, an early millwright in Lexington wrote: "Captain Newell had ordered to draft 3 or 4 from his company which included but 20 or 30 militia in the whole county—Captain Newell summons us to attend, we did attend, & it fell to the lot of Amariah Watson & Calvin Culver to be of the persons chosen to go. We wrote Captain Walker & requested him to come and see our exposed situation. He did come in company with Captain Newell to my house & both said they did not blame us for refusing to go. They thought we would have trouble guarding our own front and homes so they let us stay where we were & Captain Walker sent us seven muskets and ammunition for our defense at home. Captain Walker went with his company to Detroit & was there at Hull's surrender & left us in the woods with the Indians *(R. A. Carter, Tom Lyons The Indian Who Died 13 Times 2011, 26)."*

To their horror, Mansfielders began receiving dispatches from Sandusky detailing the loss of 150 tons of lead, 25 pieces of heavy artillery, 8 brass field guns, thousands of stands of muskets, 60 large barrels of gunpowder, a vast amount of flour and 300 head of cattle *(Langguth 2006)*. Worst of all, Hull surrendered, without terms, his 2800 men, many of them militia called-up from poorly-defended central Ohio.

Amariah Watson's younger brother Samuel was given a militia Captaincy, taking command of a hastily built blockhouse on the Clearfork just east of Bellville's Main Street bridge.

John Laylan had sailed aboard the schooner *Sally* from its home port in Cuyahoga, running victuals, clothing and munitions to Fort Detroit from the emptying supply houses that peppered the south-eastern shore of Lake Erie *(Laylan 1862, 82)*. On June 29, while the *Sally* swung at anchor in Huron, Colonel Enos came aboard reading-out the official declaration of war and taking immediate passage to Fort Maumee. Upon entering the Maumee they were fired upon by hostile war parties flying a Union Jack from their village. Some of them piled into canoes making several attempts at boarding. This they kept up until reaching Fort Maumee near dusk. At the time, all ships not flying the Union Jack were boarded, and deserters from the British navy were seized and hanged. The Henry Levering tale is an example *(Levering Family Association 1892, 112-113)*.

At dawn, with a hold partly full, the *Sally* weighed anchor and pressed on slowly for Detroit. On August 15, she drew close enough to witness Hull's capitulation. Narrowly escaping, the *Sally* made landfall at the mouth of the Chagrin River. Locals, suspecting they were British soldiers, turned on them with stones and clubs. They were beaten until a local justice figured the whole thing out. Laylan started south on foot, eventually enlisting at Mansfield in Johnson's rifle company under Enos's command, garrisoning the twin blockhouses that guarded its jittery inhabitants.

Regional instability spread as stories of Indian depredations and murders of settlers steadily trickled south, culminating in the deaths of Jones, Ruffner, the Zimmers and Copus. As an old man looking back on his life, Laylan wrote: "I enlisted in a regiment located at Mansfield, to protect the frontier. While there, a Sergeant and four men, of whom I was one, were out on a scout. After proceeding some distance, we struck a fresh trail. The Sergeant and one man followed it while the rest passed around the other side of the hill. We soon heard a gun, and hastened around, found that the other company came in sight of two Indians—had shot and scalped one and the other escaped. Upon our return to camp, forty men were sent to reconnoiter. They proceeded as near Upper Sandusky, as was prudent, and reported on their return, three or four thousand Indians there."

My version of Laylan's journey combines several old tales to give a broader picture of what was happening in the area, changing the particulars somewhat in the process. I will correct the record here in Laylan's own words.

Laylan, then a settler from Mount Vernon, worried for his family's safety. He applied for a furlough pleading that his brother-in-law had joined the regular army leaving his wife and womenfolk to fend for themselves *(Garber 2003, 126-127)*. By this time little could be spared from local arsenals as militia commanders began quarreling with their regular army counterparts over who had control of distribution of such arms as remained. Laylan was granted his furlough but not weapons, forcing him to make the trip unarmed. Fifty years later, Laylan wrote: "Some days after I received a furlough for five days to visit our family in Mount Vernon, I was not allowed to take my gun, and soon after I had passed the first blockhouse, which was five miles out, I discovered two Indians between me and it. The next blockhouse was five miles beyond on the other bank of the Clearfork of the Mohican there several rods wide. My only chance for safety was to reach that, and I ran as fast as possible, following the road while the Indians took a circuit through the woods to get ahead. Having their guns to carry hindered them and I gained. They soon left the woods, however, and then gained upon me. As I entered the stream, they were close at hand and fired as I plunged in. Luckily for me the excitement of the chase and the darkness prevented a good aim. The gun alarmed the people, and when I reached the other side I found the gates shut, with no chance to get in safely. Upon going around the other side of the house, I found a daughter of judge McCluer, the owner of the house who had been out to milk and forgotten by those inside in their haste. The next day, word was sent to Mansfield, but scouts found no Indians. I was so lame from the effects of the race, that I could not leave McCluer until the third day *(Laylan 1862)*."

Ohio settlers had good reason to fear for their lives when traveling much beyond Coffinberry and Winship's backyards. Enterprising men like the Watson brothers, Gass and McCluer were among the first to secure lots a few miles to the south along the Clearfork and its nearby trails. Soon their mills, taverns and homesteads became important stopping

167

points along the route to Mount Vernon. They built blockhouses or fortified their homes anticipating invasion by the British or a fifth column of local tribal warriors still squatting along the Clearfork and its feeder streams.

One incident that put Amariah Watson on edge was told to Robert Carter by Watson's great-great granddaughter in a phone interview from 1964, retold by students at Lexington Schools who wrote a History of Lexington, Ohio. "According to Robert Carter, Lexington historian, Watson's daughter was nearly taken by Indians. The miller made friends with the local tribes by grinding their grain. One day, when a group of Indians were visiting him, they left their papoose (baby) outside the house. The Miller's vicious (mean) pig found and killed the baby. The Indians wanted Watson's child Cynthia in exchange for the baby they had lost but Watson came up with an idea to save his child. He gave them the choice of the pig or his daughter. The Indians chose the pig, and Watson got his child back *(Pinka 2002)*."

Thieves, squatters and Natives roamed the surrounding wilderness, occasionally waylaying travelers who, like Laylan, were unable to defend themselves. Among the shadowy figures of the Clearfork valley was hot-tempered Celestial Light. He was born Evera Celeste Le Blond in France to a respectable family of some wealth, at the height of the French Revolution year of terror, March 22 1789. Le Blond was drafted into Napoleon's Grand Armeé, but before deploying he killed a man in a duel, an offense punishable by death by guillotine. Smuggled aboard a ship by his father, Le Blond sailed for Canada, packed into a hold. Sometime in 1811, he made his presence known to residents of Fredericktown, Ankneytown and Bellville. *(Norton 1862, 841-842)*. At gatherings, he would regale them with fireside stories of violent escapades, boasting that in France there was a $5000 price on his head (sometimes he doubled the figure). Frontier toughs developed a fearful respect for the touchy little Frenchman, corrupting his long name to Celestial Light, a pseudonym he happily adopted, using it in his early signatures.

Like the Watsons and McCluer, Light strove to position himself for the coming influx of settlers. He opened a hat shop in Fredericktown but went broke. Nevertheless, by the end of the war, he had mysteriously gathered enough money to build a mill which he sold uncompleted to David Shaler *(N. N. Hill 1881, 424)*. The community of Ankneytown sprang up around Shaler's Mill. Light's refined signature shows up on an 1815 roll call of Militia in Fredericktown. Enticed by the promise of free liquor, a company formed at a local tavern commanded by its owner, Captain Abner Ayers *(Hopkins n.d., 14)*.

In 1838 Light's father died leaving him a substantial inheritance, that is, if he could return to France undetected and claim it. He hid his identity and brashly secreted himself to Paris, successfully defying Parisian authorities. Returning to Ohio, he set up a comfortable life for himself and his growing family in Bellville. With his change in fortune, he opened a well-stocked general store and, for the first time in years, used his full name. He served on village council in 1842 and his son, Gidion, was Mayor of Bellville in 1848. Gidion lives on as a main character in William Stevens' 19th century novel, "The Unjust Judge."

Evera Celesin Le Blond (the spelling of his name varies greatly) died in 1851 and is buried near the top of Snake Hill, where many other pioneers and village elders rest in the old section of Bellville Cemetery. Garber wrote of Light: "Napoleon I, through his far-reaching power, may be credited with bringing to the forks of the Mohican this young Frenchman who found it difficult to adjust to a new way of life in the wilderness of America. Celestial Light retained his dignity and reserve as a gentleman and it is hoped that he retained some of his frivolous spirit and sense of humor as the years molded him into a good American *(Garber 2003, 80).*

Early in the Spring of 1818 John Laylan moved his family onto a fifty acre plot of unbroken wilderness just south of Norwalk. There, with the help of his brother Charles, he cleared and improved a substantial set of fields along what is now Laylan Road. He and his family soon prospered despite the fact that he never fully recovered his health following his nearly fatal dash to Mount Vernon. Norwalk at this time was a lawless place where residents formed armed neighborhoods, meeting in one another's homes to handle new problems that came in the post-war era. Horse thieves, counterfeiters and highwaymen scoured the countryside, robbing locals of their new-found prosperity. Many settlers abandoned their old codes of hospitality and learned to lock their doors.

In a letter to The Firelands Pioneer dated June of 1862, Laylan wrote of the times: "In the fall of 1819 there was an evening meeting appointed at Joseph Crawford's, where John Dounce now lives. Myself and family went to the meeting and shut up our house. We returned, on our way home, about ten O'Clock at night. On approaching the house, we heard a great noise within, and while endeavoring to discover the cause, a number of squaws come to us in the dark and informed us that some fifteen or twenty Indians had taken possession of the house, and had partaken largely of "firewater," and that it would not be safe for us to go to the house until they became sober; at the same time guaranteeing to us the safety of our property. So we went back to Mr. Crawford's and remained until after breakfast. In the morning when we returned home, a humbler set of beings you ever saw than those Indians were. The squaws then restored their weapons, which they had taken from them secretly to prevent bloodshed. To our surprise we found everything safe and sound."

John Laylan died in Norwalk, Ohio on April 26, 1877 *(Firelands Pioneer 1878)*. His house stood on the East side of Laylan Road just North of South Norwalk Road *(Norwalk Reflector 1933-1995, 134)*.

<u>1812 Dangers</u>

Enough has been written about Indian depredations. These stories are well known to students of pioneer history. From Colonel Brinkerhoff's truly disturbing account of the murder of Colonel Crawford, to the Victorian Ohio historians' gothic accounts of the fates of the Zimmers, Ruffner, Levi Jones and Copus, these tales have remained vivid in our view of the times *(Graham 1880, 59)*. Baughman, Graham and Howe grew up hearing these stories of atrocities, often first hand, from those who were there and remembered. Their parents and grandparents lived at a time when any retribution taken against the Indians was seen as justifiable. Baughman in his 1908 History of Richland County writes: "It is a maudlin sentimentality to dilate upon the wrongs which the white settlers committed against the Indians. For the few misdeeds that may have been done by the pioneers were too insignificant to be given prominence in history or to attempt to excuse or offset the bloody outrages committed by the Indians with the few incidental retaliations of the Whites."

The victor gets to tell the story. It is easy to forget that to be a Native in Ohio during this period was at least as perilous as being a settler. Many settlers viewed Natives as pariahs, resenting their age-old claims to hunting grounds, viewing them as another dangerous feral intruder, sometimes shooting them on sight. Every man, woman and child on the frontier knew the macabre story of the death of Colonel Crawford two decades earlier. Warriors of the Indian Chief, Captain Pipe, captured, tortured and burned Crawford alive after his defeat near Upper Sandusky. On balance, one must remember that this brutal event was in retaliation for actions of Crawford's superior who murdered the entire population of Gnadenhuten, a peaceful Indian settlement. These people were lined up and murdered one-by-one with a hammer.

But it was the specter of Colonel Crawford burning at the stake that haunted Ohioans in the summer of 1812, not the frantic pleas of Gnadenhutens's helpless population. No Native was safe. Toby, a Wyandot elder, respected by so many early settlers was not immune to murder, nor were innocent Native children. Garber gives an account of the unflinching murder of a young Delaware child: "The man was George Carpenter. He was an early settler in Doughty Valley where he entered land about one mile downstream from the site of Beck's Mills. It was upon this land that the murder occurred. Not far away an itinerant camp of Delaware Indians was located on a small stream. Carpenter was clearing his land and burning the felled timber. He had a huge fire burning one evening, when a small Indian boy ventured into the clearing hoping to find his way back to his people. The boy was lost. What motivated Carpenter can never be known, but he grabbed up the small boy, tossed him into the raging fire and watched him burn to death."

Natives who avoided removal sometimes found themselves hunted by settlers looking for trophy scalps, their lives forfeit to the individual whims of settlers and soldiers, filled with anxiety, and reeling from Hull's surrender of Fort Detroit. Anxious farmers did not know when they left for a day of toil that their families would be safe from attack by marauding warriors. In reality, many more Natives ventured into the wilderness, never to return home. Their scalps sometimes adorned the mantles and doorways of those who feared them.

Today many descendants of those original pioneers live within walking distance of where their ancestors first laid claim to land. Old cemeteries have rows of their graves. There is little that remains of the tribal populations that once flourished through the same countryside, other than traces of their DNA carried by these descendants of pioneers.

1813 and Beyond

Kanotchy languished in his cramped cell inside a dank windowless New Philadelphia, Ohio jail. He was recovering from a near fatal dose of poison that had slowly killed and sickened a number of his followers who were also made captive with him. Months earlier, he and his war party—who had been on the move since the attacks along the Blackfork—made camp on a spit of land known to locals as "Fern Island" in the Tuscarawas River *(Baughman 1908, 95)*. Captain McConnel, a local militia commander, hearing of Kanotchy's presence, marched his troops around the wooded flood plains of both river banks like deadly bookends trapping Kanotchy and his unsuspecting war party. McConnel and his men concealed themselves in dense foliage and waited for morning to come. At dawn his men formed skirmish lines on both banks of the Tuscarawas, leveling their muskets at Kanotchy's surprised warriors while McConnel swam his horse, alone, across the river's Eastern branch and demanded Kanotchy and his men's unconditional surrender. They complied *(Baughman 1908, 75)*.

The prisoners were waded ashore and bound. McConnel's men petitioned their captain to execute Kanotchy and his band where they stood, but McConnel overruled their request, deciding instead to march them to New Philadelphia for trial. There, Kanotchy and his men filled the Sheriff's jail to capacity as they awaited a form of justice many felt their race did not deserve. Mobs formed at local taverns, but their discontent was tepid at best and they only verbally accosted McConnel and his men on the streets as they went about their business.

News of Kanotchy's capture soon reached Wooster, where Captain Mullens, a local militia commander decided to march his men, without orders, to New Philadelphia with the intent of wresting Kanotchy and his followers from McConnel's custody, promising to hang the "bloodthirsty savages." Captain McConnel and Sheriff Laffer made an urgent appeal to New Philadelphians to turn out armed and repulse Mullens and his rogue force.

Only one man showed up, a visiting attorney from Steubenville named John C. Wright. He volunteered, placing himself beside McConnel and Laffer, between Mullen's men and the county jail. Baughman wrote: "Mr. Wright pleaded with the attacking party for the lives of the Indians and declared that if the prisoners were harmed it would be after they had walked over their dead bodies. The attack was finally abandoned and the company returned to Wooster."

Not long afterwards, some recruits from Newark, incensed by tales of Kanotchy's atrocities, dosed the prisoners with poison, killing a few and sickening the rest. In the throes of his illness, Kanotchy admitted to Sheriff Laffer that he was responsible for Kate Zimmer's grizzly murder along with that of Copus and Ruffner, deflecting blame from his followers *(Neel 2009, 36)*. Astonishingly, at the urging of Governor Meigs, Kanotchy and his men were turned over to authorities of the regular army where, as prisoners of war, they were released at the end of hostilities. Kanotchy never recovered his prestige or leadership and was knifed to death one year later by one of his tribesmen.

On March 31, 1813 the British General Proctor, with an invasion force of 500 regulars and 800 tribal warriors made their way to the Sandusky River in two well-armed gunboats, landing his men in the river's shallows just above Fort Stevenson in what is now greater Fremont in Sandusky County. The fort's commander, Major Croghan, had refused an order by his superior, General William Henry Harrison to withdraw and blow-up the fort, leaving nothing for the invading British. With a garrison of only 200, Croghan had that morning brashly turned away a British Lieutenant who had entered the fort under a flag of truce, expecting Croghan to surrender much in the same fashion of Hull almost a year earlier. The letter from Captain Dickson, Proctor's field commander, to Croghan brazenly smacks of Brock's threat made to Hull at Fort Detroit. It reads: "—Sir for God's sake, surrender, and prevent the dreadful massacre that will be caused by your resistance." When Croghan refused, the British replied with a heavy cannonade from Proctor's gun boats and light artillery landed by Dickson on the opposite bank. Procter kept this up, with little effect, until dawn when Dickson, after receiving another refusal to surrender, ordered a frontal assault on the fort. It was then that Croghan's heavy artillery opened-up on the tight ranks of the British, felling many of them along the fort's defensive ditch and scattering Proctor's Indian allies. Howe would later write: "Colonel Short who commanded the regulars of the forlorn hope, was ordering his men to leap the ditch, cut down the pickets, and give the Americans no quarter, when he fell, mortally wounded into the ditch, hoisted his white handkerchief on the end of his sword, and begged for the mercy that he had a moment before ordered to be denied to his enemy."

That night, fearing a counterattack from Harrison's infantry, now on the march, Proctor withdrew, leaving Colonel Short and 25 regulars dead in the ramparts ditch. Twenty-six more regulars were badly wounded and surrendered. Proctor's 800 Indian warriors were left to fend for themselves.

The next day Colonel Ball's dragoons at the vanguard of Harrison's force came under fire from concealed bands of warriors while reconnoitering outside the fort. Ball's troops soon flushed them out, cutting Proctor's abandoned warriors to pieces from horseback. Howe relates: "Lieu. Hedges (now General Hedges of Mansfield) following in the rear, mounted on a small horse, pursued a big Indian, and just as he had come up to him his stirrup broke, and he fell head-first off his horse, knocking the Indian down. Both sprang to their feet, when Hedges struck the Indian across his head, and as he was falling, buried his sword up to its hilt in his body."

Hedges would later be promoted and saw his fair share of action. After the war Hedges—one of Jared Mansfield's original "land spies"—returned to Richland County, building a fine house that stands on Park Avenue West across from the Renaissance Theatre. John Chapman was a guest in this house where he was billeted in the attic because of Mrs. Hedges's aversion to his filthy clothes and gamey aroma. As far as I know, this is the last standing structure in Mansfield known to have hosted the legendary arborist.

Hedges died on October 4, 1854, living long enough to see the overgrown hill where he once pitched his tent become a sprawling young city that, at the time, rivaled Cleveland in industry, and it could be argued, was a more crucial destination at that time than it is today.

September 10, 1813

Cloaked in wispy morning fog, Tecumseh paddled his canoe, alone, through the glassy water of another windless morning on Lake Erie, some miles from the towering black silhouettes of Commodore Perry's fleet, where scores of sailors in longboats strained hard at their oars, bringing the squadron's heavy guns to bear on the British fleet that lay becalmed near the Bass Islands.

A few days earlier, Tecumseh and the British naval commander, Robert Barclay, made a grand tour of the squadron, dining aboard Barclay's flagship, the *Detroit* (her name was no doubt a jab at Hull's surrender). Tecumseh was much taken by the young fighting captain, one of Admiral Nelson's favorite officers who, eight years earlier, had lost an arm at the battle of Trafalgar. Tecumseh, unlike many of his fellow chieftains understood the need for naval dominance of Lake Erie as a logistical necessity for supplying the men and equipment necessary to regain control of Ohio and its surrounding territories.

At 7:00 am Barclay's topmen sighted the makeshift American fleet. As the wind slowly picked-up, Barclay spied Perry's flagship, the *U.S.S. Lawrence* through his glass. When in range the *Detroit* unleashed a murderous broadside that tore into the newly built *Lawrence* which sailed boldly ahead of the American fleet. The *Lawrence* hove-to and returned equally devastating fire as British shot tore away most of *Lawrence's* bulwarks and rigging, reducing her to a sinking hulk. Although crippled and taking on water, *Lawrence's* great guns battered the *Detroit* at close-range, riddling the frigate's unseasoned hull, killing many of Barclay's crew. Barclay, wounded five times, collapsed from blood loss and was carried below. His men, chiefly made up of Canadian farmers, a few sailors, and a number of Tecumseh's warriors, fumbled around their gun positions, severely concussed and slipping in blood that now washed the *Detroit's* splintered gun deck. Later, at his court martial, Barclay would claim that Tecumseh's warriors fled in terror to the hold after witnessing a deck hand cut-in-two by enemy shot. This, he claimed, greatly reduced his fighting strength.

Aboard *Lawrence's* slower consort, the sloop *U.S.S Scorpion*, John Rice, a pioneer from Richland County and recent volunteer, resisted the urge to vomit from anxiety, concentrating on manning his station on one of Scorpion's big forward guns, the operation of which, like the sloop itself, was alien to him. A soldier in Harrison's army, Rice had volunteered for the chance to earn prize money and a cash bounty. These enticements were most welcome at a time when frontier soldiers were unlikely to receive even their regular pay. In later years at his home in Shelby, he would recall to anyone who would listen, details of the hellish firefight the *Scorpion* sailed into, as Perry transferred his flag from the shattered *Lawrence* to her formidable sister ship the *Niagra*, which defeated Barclay in what became one of the great fleet actions in naval history.

Midway through the battle, Tecumseh turned his canoe around, unable to see through swirling clouds of thick black smoke and haze which hung like a drape over the vicious contest. The slowing rate of muzzle flashes from Barclay's direction told him all he needed to know of the great loss.

Rice, like Harrison, Hedges, Proctor, and Tecumseh would clash once more, on foot, at the battle of the Thames, three months later. John Rice died at his home in 1880 in Shelby, Ohio the last documented veteran of the battle of Lake Erie.

The battle of the Thames and its consequences.

An honored guest of General Harrison, Commander Perry, brought his horse to a slow trot, passing a column of U. S. regulars as they marched double-time towards their forward positions before the inevitable assault. Through his glass, Perry studied Harrison's objectives with a mixture of curiosity and concern. General Proctor—a man with nothing left to lose after his disastrous assault on Fort Stevenson—sat straight as a ramrod upon a magnificent white horse, addressing his staff on high ground not a half mile away. From the distant tree line that flanked Proctor and his infantry came howls and whoops of an unknown number of warriors guided by Tecumseh himself.

At Harrison's side, Captain Richard M. Johnson argued with his brother, James over leadership of the "forlorn hope," a veritable suicide charge intended to keep Tecumseh's warriors from supporting Proctor's infantry once the contest had begun. For once, the Commodore was happy to be a mere observer, leaving the coming battle to men like Harrison, Johnson, and the fearsome volunteers from Ohio and Kentucky, whom he personally admitted were little different from the savages they faced. Perry, now the darling of the American press, had already secured his place in history.

As for Harrison and Johnson, the next half hour would also lay the foundations of their rise to power in post-war American politics. John Rice would later claim to have personally witnessed Tecumseh's demise at the hands of Richard Johnson, an act that made Johnson as famous as Harrison *(Garber 2003, 294)*. Soon after Tecumseh fell, Proctor, overwhelmed by Harrisons forces, fled the field of battle with his guard, leaving those who could not follow to fend for themselves. All hope for a tribal confederacy gaining a sovereign territory dwindled rapidly following the death of Tecumseh. Native Americans seen in any numbers throughout Ohio became a rarity outside of small government controlled reservations, the last of which at Upper Sandusky became nothing more than a ruined church and cemetery—which restored, remains to this day a time capsule—as its population was pushed West.

The end of the war saw an explosion in business in Mansfield. A great influx of settlers and entrepreneurs traveled the hundreds of miles of roads—crude and often nearly impassable—carved out by Harrison's armies. Through these arteries streamed trade from ports on the Great Lakes, south to transport houses along the Ohio River. Most of it travelled through Mansfield's expanding footprint. Although the risk of Indian attack had passed, predation by wildlife remained a problem. Around Mansfield, dangerous animals roamed the land. Wolves were common on the periphery of town stalking those unlucky enough to conclude their business after dark. Bears also abounded frequently clashing with locals *(Baughman 1908, 25)*.

Mansfield H. Glikison recalled: "Stephen Curran went out one day, near the spring, to make clapboards, and, while he was at work, left his dinner on a stump. Happening to look in the direction of the stump during his labor, he saw a large black bear helping himself to his dinner. Curran, finding he could not scare the bruin away by yelling at him, attacked him with an ax. The bear showed fight, but Curran was also plucky, and the bear beat a retreat; but ran directly towards the public square, where he was overtaken by Curran, who seized him by the tail. The Irishman had, in the meantime, been making considerable noise, and quite a crowd had collected. The bear whirled rapidly about, Curran holding the tail for some time, until his hold slipping, he was thrown several feet away, and notwithstanding the crowd, or, very likely, because of it, the bear ran away down the ravine behind the North American and escaped eventually *(Graham 1880, 461)*." A grand hunt was formed in 1828, and another in 1846. Hundreds of wolves, wildcats and bears and dens of snakes were killed, their numbers dwindling to a memory by the century's end.

General Proctor, recalled to England in disgrace, died at his ancestral home, a broken man, in 1815. In 1836 Richard Johnson ran for the Vice Presidency supporting Democrat Martin Van Buren. They won using the popular Ohio and Kentucky jingle "Rumsey dumpsey, Rumsey dumsey, Richard Johnson killed Tecumseh." Unfortunately for Johnson and ultimately Van Buren, the aging war hero's term ended in disaster in 1840 over allegations that Johnson had an African American slave as a common-law wife. Van Buren ran for re-election without Johnson and lost to William Henry Harrison. The hero of Tippicanoe and the battle of the Thames, completed his resume as President of the United States, only to die in office from complications of pneumonia, serving only one month as commander in chief.

Richard Johnson, so revered in Ohio, passed away in 1850, two weeks into his first term in the Kentucky House of Representatives.

James Purdy settled with his family in Richland County shortly after the war. Later in life he wrote of the times: "The early settlers were without transportation for their grain part of which was worked up into whiskey and sent by way of Sandusky to Detroit and sold to the Indians to assist in their civilization. Furs, pelts, gentian, smoked hams, and rags were taken in trade by Mansfield's merchants and sent to Pittsburg in four-horse wagons."

From the brickyard where Levi Jones was scalped by Indians came the material for new buildings. Their facades and spires had, by 1830 replaced nearly all traces of 1812 Mansfield from its square. By 1815 Dr. Royal V. Powers, Mansfield's first permanent physician, had Jones's old shop leveled, replacing the crude log structure with a fine two-story brick office and home. His sister and receptionist would later marry Millard Fillmore. Within a decade, this building would be replaced with grander, more modern edifices, culminating with the sprawling Reeds building in 1865, which is now the oldest building on the square.

Unfortunately, George McCullough's war did not end with the Treaty of Ghent in 1815. Gilkison told of meeting him on the road to Upper Sandusky around 1820 (The Delaware Reservation was still there). He was dressed as an Indian and armed to the teeth. When asked what his intentions were, McCullough answered that he was "going to hunt Indians." In later years, McCullough would become a staunch unionist, and oddly for his character, a vehement abolitionist, living into old age. McCullough died peacefully in 1866 and was buried on his family's farm near Mount Vernon.

Remembered as eccentric and foppish, Winn Winship retained his position as postmaster until 1820 when, after losing a bid to become Representative in the Ohio House, he received a commission in the army, temporarily leaving Mansfield, to command the 4th Ohio Regiment. In 1829 he returned to the rapidly growing town, adding his name with a flourish to Mansfield's newly formed fire company charter. Later he would serve as commissioner of the Richland Huron Bank. Garber wrote: "Winship had been maligned by personal criticism which stemmed from differences in background and environment. Unkind references to his fastidiousness in personal and eating habits serve to contrast the living conditions where he first lived with the privacy which he preferred. The known popularity which he enjoyed must be accepted as removing the sting from these unkind illusions *(Garber 2003, 68)*." Sometime in the late 1840s Winship left Ohio for good, disappearing from the record. What became of this founding pioneer remains unknown.

John Gilkison had a varied career after his return to civilian life. His father-in-law, George Coffenberry had published a newspaper in Lancaster, Ohio called *"The Olive Branch."* Gilkison published Mansfield's first newspaper, *"The Olive"* in 1818. It was a single page broadside that Coffinberry often read aloud, as well as any letters that happened to be nailed to Winship's mail post.

Gilkison was appalled by Mansfield's first schoolmaster, a cruel, inept drunk. He sold his interest in the *Olive*—while remaining as printer — and became the new township schoolmaster, with the backing of Hedges. At first, he ran his school from the front parlor of Mrs. Coffinberry's house, but after some months and at the urging of Mrs. Coffinberry, Gilkison and others built a one room schoolhouse on land provided by Hedges (saving much wear and tear on Mrs. Coffinberry's furnishings).

Gilkison's son, Mansfield Gilkison, later admitted that his father was a poor school teacher, a career he relinquished to more talented people. He returned to the press in 1823 with *"The Mansfield Gazette,"* a politically driven paper dubbed the *"Gilkisonian"* by those who disliked it. He went on to become Mayor of Mansfield from 1827 to 1835 and died in 1856 at the age of 70, a much respected city father.

Illustrations

The front cover is a montage of the author's photographs. Other illustrations were reproduced, or composed from elements found in 19th century publications noted below. The back cover is a montage based on Sears, Robert 1845 fig 55.

Works Cited

Barnes, A. S., & Co. 1875. *A Popular History of the United States of America*. New York, New York : A. S. Barnes & Co.

Baughman, A. J. 1908. *History of Richland County Ohio from 1808-1908*. Chicago, IL: S. J. Clarke Publishing Co.

Berton, Pierre. 1980. *The Invasion of Canada, 1812-1813*. Toronto, Ontario: McClelland and Stewart.

Brinkerhoff, Roeliff. 1993. *A Pioneer History of Richland County*. Edited by Mary Jane Henney. Mansfield, OH: Richland County Chapter, Ohio Genealogical Society.

Carter, Robert A. and Cullen, Michael C. 2016. *Water Powered Mills of Richland County*. Tauras Publishing.

Carter, Robert A. 2007. *Tales of the Old-Timers: The History of Lexington*. Ashland, OH: Privately Printed.

—. 2011. *Tom Lyons The Indian Who Died 13 Times*. Reprinted by the Greentown Preservation Association. Published by Robert A. Carter.

Cunningham, Margaret. 1873. "Letter of Margaret Cunningham." *Mansfield Shield and Banner*, Jan 31.

Duff, Wiliam. 1931. *History of North Central Ohio Embracing Ashland, Wayne, Medina, Lorain, Huron, Richland and Knox Counties*. Vol. Volume 1. Topeka-Indianapolis: Historical Publishing.

Firelands Pioneer. 1878. "Obituary of John Laylan." *Firelands Pioneer*, July.

Garber, Dwight Wesley. 2003. *Tales of the Mohican.* Edited by comp. by Mary Jane Henney. Mansfield, OH: Richland County Genealogical Society.

Graham, A. A. 1880. *History of Richland County, Ohio.* Mansfield, OH: A. A. Graham Publishers.

Greentown Preservation Association. 2018. *Home Page (accessed 2/15/18).* http://www.greentownpreservation.org.

Harbaugh, Thomas C., ed. 1909. *Centennial History Troy, Piqua, and Miami County, Ohio and Representative Citizens.* Chicago, IL: Richmond-Arnold Publishing Co.

Hill, George William, M. D. 1880. *History of Ashland County, Ohio, With Illustrations and Biographical Sketches.* Cleveland, OH: Williams bros.

Hill, N. N. Jr. 1881. *History of Knox County, Ohio. Its Past and Present...* Mount Vernon, Ohio: A. A. Graham & Co.

Hopkins, James Robert. n.d. *Knox Folklore and Fact.* Mount Vernon, Ohio.

Howe, Henry. 1907. *Historical Collections of Ohio in Two Volumes.* Ohio Centennial Edition. 2 vols. Cincinnati, OH: C. J. Krehbiel & Co.

Johnson, H. U. 1894. *From Dixie to Canada Romances and Realities of the Underground Railroad.* Buffalo: Charles Wells Moulton.

Kaufman, Paul H. 1973. *Indian Lore of the Muskingum Headwaters of Ohio.*

Knapp, H. S. 1863. *A History of the Pioneer and Modern Times of Ashland County, from the Earliest to the Present Date.* Philadelphia, PA: J. R. Lippincott.

Langguth, A. J. 2006. *Union 1812, the Americans Who Fought the Second War of Independence.* New York: Simon and Schuster.

Laylan, John. 1862. "Recollections of Pioneer Life." *The Fire Lands Pioneer*, 84.

Levering Family Association. 1892. *Proceedings of the Levering Family Reunion held at Levering, Knox County, Ohio August 6, 1891.* Columbus, Ohio: J. L. Trauger, Book and Job Printer.

Levison, Mary Eileen Schuler. 1908. *Ohio was Their Home.* Bellville, OH: Richland County Genealogical Society, 2008.

Mansfield Shield and Banner. 1873. "Letter of Margaret Cunningham." Jan 31.

Moorehead, Warren King. 1899. *The Indian Tribes of Ohio.* Facsimile reprint, 1992. Edited by Arthur W. McGraw. Ohio archaeological and historical publications.

Neel, Thomas Stephen. 2009. *Greentown: a story of 1812 in contemporary documents.* Ashland, OH: Ashland County Chapter, Ohio Genealogical Society.

Norton, A. Banning. 1862. *History of Knox County, Ohio, From 1779 to 1862 Inclusive.* Columbus, OH: Richard Nevins.

Norwalk Reflector. 1933-1995. "Just Like Old Times."

Ohio Register. 1812. "Death Notice." *Ohio Register*, Aug 10.

Pinka, Sharon and Ferguson, Amy Gratz, ed. 2002. *Looking Back at Lexington. A History of the Village of Lexington, Ohio 1813-2002.* Lexington, Ohio: Lexington Junior High School.

Price, Robert. 1967. *Johnny Appleseed, Man and Myth.* Glouster, Mass.: P. Smith.

Sears, Robert. 1845. *The Pictorial History of the American Revolution ; With a Sketch of the Early History of the Country, the Constitution of the United States, and a Chronological Index. .* New York, New York: Robert Sears.

Shea, John Gilmary, LL.D. 1886. *The Story of A Great Nation. or Our Country's Achievements, Military, Naval, Political and Civil.* New York, New York: Gay Brothers & Co.

Taylor, Alan. 2010. *The Civil War of 1812: American extras, British subjects, Irish rebels & Indian allies.* New York, NY: Alfred A. Knopf.

Trautman, Milton Bernhard. 1981. *Fishes of Ohio: with illustrated keys.* Columbus: Ohio State University Press.

Made in the USA
Columbia, SC
11 November 2024

45741288R00121